A Letter from the Author

Growing up, I was all over the place. I didn't know what I wanted to do in life other than write. I have been actively writing since I was ten years old. I started writing poetry, then short stories, then I moved on to songwriting. Even when I felt lost, I always fell back on some form of writing.

When I began this book, I never would have thought I would finish it. When going through a hard time, or whenever I came to a block in the road, I would try different things that made me feel liberated. Writing this book started out as an outlet to escape the outside world. In the beginning stages, I would write then stop for months, then I would start again, and stop for even longer. Then finally one day I really sat and thought to myself, "I can do this." I think I may have written a total of five chapters at that point and then I finished the rest within six months.

Well, as great as everything seemed, I ended up losing the last half of my book and had to rewrite the entire thing, which in turn was a great thing. I am a strong believer in things happening the way they should. I feel like the universe was telling me that what I wrote previously wasn't right. I was upset at first, feeling like I wasted time and effort that I couldn't get back. But then I thought about it more in depth. Rewriting the end of my book could be a beautiful thing, and it was.

The moral of the story is this: When you are passionate about something, stick to it. No matter how long it takes you, no matter what happens, no matter the road blocks or the distance ahead. Everything will work out the way it is supposed to, the way it is meant to. Don't be discouraged. Don't quit. You have a story to tell. No matter how easy or difficult it is, it must be told.

—

To my first love:

I wrote this book right before I fell deeply in love with you. We were bad for each other in so many ways. Without you, this book wouldn't even exist. You broke me down and forced me to rebuild myself to be better and stronger than ever. Even throughout all the bad things that did transpire during our run, you pushed the fuck out of me and I will always love you for that. You made a lot of this possible, headache and all. I appreciate you. This piece of me is not solely reflected on my life, but without my experiences with you, I would have never come to write anything this close to my heart. So real, so raw, and so personal. Again, thank you.

To my beloved cousin:

I know you're smiling down on me right now. I finally found my way. I'm sorry I haven't taken the time out to find you in my dreams recently, but I do feel you here with me daily. I know I'm never alone. Who knew such a beautiful tragedy would inspire such a vivid creation. You are all throughout these pages. You were with me every step of the way. And I know you'll continue to be with me throughout my entire journey. I love you. I dedicate this book to your life and more importantly, your legacy. You didn't have the chance to showcase all your work the way you wanted to, but as long as I live, I will be a greater artist for not only myself, but for you as well.

To Keshell:

I can't begin to put into words how much you have helped me and been in my corner throughout this project. I just want you to know that my love for you is infinite. Not only are you one of my biggest supporters, you're one of my best friends. If I need something, you come right away, no questions asked. Thank you for taking such a huge part in something so personal to me. You don't have to do half of the things that you do for me, but you do it all out of love and I will always remember that. I love you. This is forever.

To my current lover:

Over this short time that we have been dealing, you've taught me more about myself than any man I've ever dealt with. You've taught me true sincerity, patience (not with you but with myself), communication, and that I am worth way more than what modern day society thinks I am. You will forever be my friend. The most important thing you've taught me is to heal. I will always be broken if I don't rebuild and move forward. The things about me that I thought I could never change are all being changed. I don't even think you realize how important you are to me. "Say what you mean and mean what you say." That's one of the realest things you've taught me. You've been on my ass about this book since the first time I've mentioned it to you. You saw something in me that I couldn't see yet, and for that, I thank you. No matter where you and I end up, you will always be close to my heart.

CHAPTER ONE

I crossed my left leg behind my right, as I always have when facing uneasiness. The pointed heels that were drawn on my feet were a reminder that I was still a young professional and was well respected by not only my professor, but by my peers. With the position that I held, you would think this feeling would seldom cross my path. To be honest, the feeling of nervousness should no longer be familiar to me at all. This was just a college assignment, it's not like I was telling Dale my true feelings about him. It wasn't like this was a conversation with someone important. This whole, "Read Between the Lines," speech was a little mediocre to me personally.

This was my last year as a film major at the University of Cincinnati. To receive my financial aid, I had to be a full-time student, so I took this philosophy class just to make sure my schedule was up to par. It would be an easy GPA booster, I thought. But this class has been a drag and waste of my time. Instead of working on my scripts and pursuing my film career, I spent time studying and preparing for the assignments for this class.

Looking around the auditorium, majority of the seats were filled. The attention of the crowd was on me. Stepping up to the microphone, I took one more look at my surroundings. The details of each individual face weren't so visible, and that eased my nerves. Opening my mouth slightly, I fixed my stance, and began. The words began to flow, as if they had been imprisoned inside of me years before my birth.

"Often times, I feel insane because my mind and thought process are racing a mile a second. Taking strolls in the park alone, not only do I almost lose myself in the greenery, but in the very footsteps that are taken. They say that the average creative individual talks to themselves often. Those same people say that the unusual individual *needs* time alone, otherwise they won't function properly. *They* say that it's normal. What doesn't sit well is how something can be normal to someone who isn't even considered ordinary. Who's to say that we talk to ourselves enough? We get so caught up in the real world, that is, the world that we rarely have time to get away from. And what's real to *us* is lost. There is no life without imagination. There is no truth in ourselves. The logic that we all live by isn't reality. The history that we know, the history that we were taught, is a lie.

"So that begs the question, 'Is it possible to live without a purpose?' My ancestors didn't plan for my life to be in America. I wouldn't be breathing if two or more different races didn't melt into the finest pot and mold together to create me. I myself was not taken from my village and brought to an unfamiliar place, someone's grandmother and grandfather were. One of your mothers was tossed off that ship so that mine could barely fit, so that hundreds of years later a child by the name of Noel could live and be so lost in her own life that sometimes she questions it. It all just seems so unreal at times. There are so many unanswered questions. I dig myself in too deep every time I think about it, which makes me feel way too open. It makes me feel lost because when an emotion surfaces, it doesn't resonate with me. Not every cloud has a silver lining, and every storm doesn't end with a rainbow. Every life doesn't have a purpose, a meaningful one at least. Every struggle doesn't hold beauty, and that alone must be determined individually. Beauty is in the eye of the beholder. See how easy it is to get walked around in a circle? How easy it is to let the conversation, your mind, and thought process be redirected. Case rested. I am nothing near your average human being. I bear the gene of creativity. I consist of unique physical, mental, and emotional features. I am me."

Deep breath. The speech was over. The aching in my heart though, not so much. I just poured out all my emotions in a public room to strangers who probably didn't give two shits about me, let alone what I was rambling on about. Nobody really understands art in the same way that the artist creates it, but that wasn't what had my heart aching. Looking up ever so suddenly, I saw someone so familiar to me standing near the entrance of the room. He had long, neat locs that came down to the middle of his back. His skin was brown with an orange tint, he'd always say he was golden. I loved that about him. His skin, so smooth and desirable. His arms, muscular and big. Every time I looked at him, I fell in love all over again. He looked me in the eyes and stole my soul. In that moment the auditorium was empty, there was only him and I. Gazing into his eyes took me back to last night. I risked it all and I was reminded of every detail. Looking right at the man I laid next to the night before, I felt a sense of understanding. My heart ached because even with the little bit of understanding my performance gave him, he still didn't quite get me. He still couldn't read between the lines. In many ways, I'm open, but there's a lot more that doesn't immediately come to the surface. Soon, his presence was right before me, and all the memories from last night blocked my vision. The world stood still. Amid all of the clapping and shouting from the audience, last night's story unraveled. The present moment disappeared, and the recent past was being lived again.

—

It was almost like I didn't have a heart because there was no heavy beating that usually came with this eerie feeling. I wasn't afraid or frightened; we shared this familiar moment a few times before. It was just something about this specific time that caught me off guard. There were so many things that should have been said, so many confessions that needed to come to light. But instead, there we were, naked, raw, and sensual. Every kiss he planted on my body reminded me of how much I wanted a family, and why everything we were doing right now was wrong in every way. In my body, birth control didn't exist. Telling truths didn't either, for he wasn't aware that the birth control pill packages were being tossed in the trash.

Every twirl of his tongue reminded me that I was supposed to come forth and express the overflowing ounces of love I had for him and confess that I knew about the other girl he still fucked from time to time. I had every intention to tell him that I knew all about Trinitee. I was jealous and wanted him to cut all ties with her, or I would be leaving him and conveniently forgetting about our history. But when he put me up against the wall and looked me in my eyes, everything was lost. Only time my lips separated was to kiss him back. I took control for a while, slid down on the wall, and took in what was officially mine. His head lifted, he stood strong and firm. He loved when I took control. He let out a quiet moan and ran his fingers through my hair. He never told me, but I could tell that he was infatuated with my natural curls. It was quiet, I didn't moan, I let the sounds of my tongue fill his ears until he let out another moan but this time, louder. "Damn Noel," he said, and grabbed my hair tight like he was about to put it in a ponytail. Every stroke of my tongue sparked more of a desire in another place.

Neither of us could wait to be body to body, but I teased myself a while longer until the torture could no longer be tolerated. I made it about me. I knew that he wanted to get to it but instead, I toyed with his patience, like he toyed with mine every night when he stayed out late or didn't come home. Taking my last big slurp, making sure to leave a lasting impression, I seductively crawled into the bed with my ass in the air. He flipped me over to missionary and slowly slid in. The thousandth time felt like the very first time. Every stroke gave me hope. He made me wild. The slightest rub and the slightest touch boosted my arousal. I felt myself dripping down my leg in between my thighs. Between the kisses and long licks on my breast and my neck, my mind begged the question, was our flame being rekindled? He was the one that was lost, my loyalty remained through it all. I would walk around the house like a mistress, day after day, crying because my man was off with some other woman. And when he would finally drag his ass home, he'd lay me down and love on me, making me forget that I was even mad or upset. This was our routine. I was comfortable, and the sex sealed the envelope. I didn't care that he wasn't coming home anymore because he was here with me now. I wasn't about to sabotage this feeling.

When it was time for him to release, every drop was felt. It was warm and comforting. We were back to normal as we laid body to body, heat to heat, together all night. No rounds, that one time was good enough for him to roll over and whisper, "I love you" in between kisses. I rubbed his head until he snored, the sweat on his face dried in the wind from our ceiling fan. That night, my heart was placed back in my chest. I began to feel again. While we were asleep, my heart was pumping vigorously. I was walking on water enriched with good faith. But the feeling invested in me last night, unfortunately wasn't here today.

—

He smiled at me as he approached. "You never cease to amaze me," he said, as he handed me flowers. I was quiet and appreciative. A bunch of white carnations and a few yellow tiger lilies, my favorite. Ironically, the carnation flower was a symbol of motherhood. I thanked him and welcomed him into my open arms. He didn't say much else, he just stared into my eyes, kissed me on the forehead, and told me he had to run back to work, he left early just to be here for me. It's crazy how right after dropping a bomb, he followed up with a guilt trip. He knew I didn't want him to go so he said he had to be back at work. I nodded and told him that I understood.

"Hey, stop that frowning girl," he said, noticing my smile drop from my face. His voice was soft and calm, it reminded me of my father's. When he took a breath, there was a light whistling sound, also like my sperm donor. I don't remember much about him, but those two details never left my memory.

Maybe that was why I was so attracted to Dale. Maybe that was why I didn't want to let him go. He kissed my forehead again, then tilted my chin up and met my lips with his.

"I have to go babe." I nodded, then he left. There I was, standing all alone with the flowers he presented to me. The room was full, but I felt empty. This was all too familiar. Unfortunately, I dealt with it continuously. Nothing would change, so neither would he. It was in my best interest to go ahead and purchase an emergency contraceptive, because even though I wanted everything to magically fix itself, it wouldn't. I made my decision and ran with it. No looking back, no regrets.

CHAPTER TWO

Being a personal assistant was never really a goal of mine, a self-made boss was more like it. But every CEO was an employee at one point in time, right? *Ha!* Wrong. There are at least 100 people who were just born in this shit. Like the Egyptians and all the ancient queens and kings, and the royal dynasties. They just so happened to get a cheat sheet to life, one that I wish I had at this moment. Running errands for my boss (a complete asshole) and doing the little things that she never has time do wasn't exactly my forte. I wasn't of any royal dynasty; my family was dirt poor. We had no money and

I wanted to change that. I was going to change that. So, I did what I had to do to get there and earn the position of the historic people that were born into fortune, only in this case, I'd work for every penny. I wanted to create a dynasty of my own for the next generation of my bloodline. The bad habits and financial misfortune would end with me.

Every time the fact that I was supposed to be a CEO in training was brought to my boss Tisa's attention, and Lord knows it was brought up too often, there was some bullshit ass rebuttal about why she felt I wasn't ready and didn't qualify for the type of gatherings, meetings, private parties, meet and greets, and events that she attended. The crazy thing about all this is, as much as I do for her, we were damn near in a relationship. I stuck around and dealt with every bit of it, hoping for a better outcome. I was praying that I'd learn something, possibly meet someone special or worth knowing, maybe make a new friend, or eventually be invited to one of those private parties and have the opportunity to network. Oh, the limitless possibilities. Maybe one day.

As my days grew longer, I sat and envied the individuals that didn't have to work for the things they had. The people that were born into riches, financial stability, and the status to come up in the world. There was always the possibility that they did work to be this way, in their previous lifetime. That made me more accepting of the fact that we had different grinds. Maybe their past lives were filled with gore and hurt, or maybe they spent their entire lives in search of everything they now have this go around. OK, I couldn't be mad at that. I respected it. So, I calmed down and thanked the universe that I was even in the position that I was in. My boss wasn't even that bad, she just was anal about little shit and was hard on me. She says it's because she sees the potential in me, but sometimes I honestly feel like it's because she's alone and has nothing better to do.

"Hey, are you Noel?"

I looked up from the book that I had started reading an hour or so ago, so that I could drift away in my thoughts. The man before me was dark and handsome. He had on a black button down, black slacks, and his beard was thick, healthy, and evenly distributed on his face. His skin was rich chocolate and his eyes were dark and mysterious. They were big and round; very expressive. They made me feel like I was the center of his attention. Something about him made me nervous. I found myself staring at his perfect lips, they were plump and symmetrical. A beauty mark sat right above his mustache under his nose. I sat my book down. There were way too many thoughts that would have to be put aside to continue reading. My thoughts were centered around taking a Plan B pill last night after my speech and drifting off to sleep alone. Now my attention was a victim of theft and fixed on this attractive unfamiliar man that stood in front of me. If the reaction of seeing him unexpectedly didn't show on my face then, I'm certain he thought I was a very nice, attentive woman.

"That would be me," I said. "How can I be of service?"

The tall, dark, and very attractive man looked me straight in the eyes as if he wasn't expecting to see so deep into my soul, like he saw beneath all the makeup and hard exterior. Keeping composure, I asked again with a little more sarcasm.

"Was there something that I could possibly assist you with Mr... Davis?"

There was a name written on the top of his folders that he had bunched in his left hand. I couldn't see the first name, but Davis was written nice and neat in red.

"Apologies, I was just a little distracted. Um yes, I'm looking to find a desk just like the one you're stationed at. Tisa told me to talk to you and you would be able to tell me everything that I needed to know about my position and where I would be during most of the day. I'm a personal assistant. Sorry, I should have told you that initially." He extended his hand for a shake.

I guess he could tell by the look on my face that I wasn't pleased by the information that he just provided. Before any assumptions were made, I cleared my throat slightly and responded.

"Ah yes, the personal assistants usually sit here when we're not busy or being summoned. What's your name? Your first name I mean. Sincerest apologies, I can't really read between the lines that well." I tried to get a better look at his whole name that lay on his bright red folder. I saw his hand still extended and shook it.

"Davis." A smirk appeared across his lips. So, I'm not sure what kind of fucking idiot he thinks I am or what type of fool Tisa takes me for, but I'm not dealing with this today. I'm more than certain Tisa didn't need another personal assistant. She's just starting to take off and her budget isn't that established yet. So, it's looking like he's here to replace me.

"Nice name. I'll be right back." I quickly got up from my desk. It was a joke that wasn't amusing at all. Clearly his first name wasn't Davis and clearly Tisa had lost her mind. Marching into Tisa's office, everything that I had to say was written on my face.

Tisa was a lighter brown complexion, lighter than me but not red boned. She didn't have a golden tint though, she was more of a cool brown, sort of ashy. Her hair was kinky, long, and healthy. She pointed at her chair, her natural nails were painted black and cut square shaped. Her fingers were slim and long, elegant and precise. But I wasn't really in the mood to take orders, so I just got to the point.

"So, apparently I'm unemployed as of today? I mean really Tisa, that was some nerve of you sending that man up to my station telling him I'll tell him all about his new job. I am offended in so many ways! Was there going to be a notice? I mean, if you didn't want me here, I would have just stayed home. I don't typically stay where I'm not wanted."

Flipping the hair out of her face, she just continued notating her work as if no one was there. My legs grew tired from standing and reflecting on how much of a fool I appeared to be, so I sat down. Rule number one: Stay composed and professional, always. Well, that rule was just broken. Rule number two: Act as a lady and not with an attitude. Is reciting rule number three necessary, because that one was broken as soon as I barged in her office. I was thinking too much and had been in her office way too long and have gotten nowhere. It felt like five whole minutes passed without her even looking in my direction. The longest five minutes of my life. But I couldn't leave. I walked into her office like I ran shit, so I had to wait for a response. Running was weak. Even though I was humiliated, I had to stick it out and deal with the consequences of my actions.

"You're being promoted, Noel, and I'm sure you know what I have to say about the actions that you just portrayed, so

I'll just save you the fuss to say this; I don't ever want to see you like that again. Now if you don't mind, go introduce yourself to that nice young man, as the lady I taught you to be. His name is Clayton. Make him feel welcome and show him the ropes. Oh, and you're welcome." She smiled at me and looked back down at her work.

Tisa was like the mom I never had. Graceful and relaxed, but she meant business. When she spoke, you could assume it was important. She was stern and gave me tough love. I knew that her intentions were pure, but she irritated me, I won't lie. I wanted her to lighten up a bit and stop being so serious all the time. I often wondered what she went through in life that made her this way.

"Tisa?" I stood up and stopped in the doorway. She just looked up at me. "What's my new position?"

A few seconds passed before she answered. "My one and only Direct Communications Specialist. I'll brief you with more information tomorrow. For the remainder of the day, take care of Clayton, please."

I nodded and left her office. Completely mortified, I remembered rule number three of the golden rules that Tisa taught me: Never show emotion. Although, the rule was broken just a few minutes prior, there was a new beginning with this Clayton guy. A clean slate. He saw none of my actions and he was just as much of a virgin to me as I was to him.

"Clayton, allow me to reintroduce myself, I'm Ms. Noel Gray. It'll be my pleasure to show you around and get you acclimated."

His pearly whites blasted through his dark lips, something I quickly grew fond of. Ignoring his laughter, I composed my skirt and grabbed his hand. He was calm and laid back, but something told me that inside he was a little nervous. As a woman, sensing when someone was attracted to me wasn't that hard. He basically was drooling over me. He seemed to be intentionally obvious with his attraction and it appeared he was trying to figure me out. He never told me how old he was, but I could tell that he was older than me. He gave me early thirties vibes. I'm sure he knew what type of woman I was, he had probably dealt with my type before. He probably thought that I was predictable. My job was to prove him wrong. Although he was very attractive, Lord knows I love proving people wrong.

Taking his pointer finger and separating it from the rest, I dipped it in the ink pad and placed it on a clean sheet of paper under the written instructions on the left side of me. All of Tisa's employees had to get a background check.

"Now, if you just take a walk down that hall, the third door on the right is a bathroom where you can wash your hands."

Without a word, he got up and did as he was told. It was something about this man that intrigued me, but I couldn't put my finger on it. That was enough to equally aggravate me and blow me away. I called myself a people reader, so for me to not be able to read him easily insulted my intelligence. That didn't make me so happy. My attraction to him slowly turned into a weird envious feeling.

Throughout the day, I caught myself locking eyes with him from time to time. It was weird, but not awkward like I imagined it to be. This situation was far from the usual. Typically, there would be a mutual interest, some eye contact, or something, but it was all just coming from me. As the day grew shorter, I dreaded leaving Tisa's office, longing to come back the next day to see him. I felt like I was in high school again and he was my crush that made me want to earn a perfect attendance award. He sparked my interest and it caught me off guard. But I wasn't the only one that was caught off guard, someone else noticed my sudden interests.

—

Dale picked me up from work and was more than a little thrown off from my great spirits.

"Baby, did something happen at work today that's got you all wired up?"

I shook my head and looked away. I wouldn't dare tell him about Clayton. Didn't need that type of drama in my life, especially since being a private investigator was my side job. I was still trying to figure out if he was stepping out on me with this Trinitee bitch. There was no room for double standards so there was no way he could have any suspicion of anything. I gave him a kiss and gazed out the window the rest of the way home, completely forgetting about the promotion that I earned earlier that day. But I guess that worked in my favor because telling him about the promotion would mean telling him about the man who took my place. Without lying to him, the choice to not tell him was the best option. He stopped the car at the top of our driveway.

"You sure you're OK?"

I nodded before I spoke. "Yes, why do you keep asking?"

I was aggravated. I wasn't upset with him, I was still thinking about Clayton. He opened his door and got out without responding to me. Straggling behind the husky love of my life, I suddenly felt all the pain in my ankles that was ignored today. I admired Dale's broad shoulders, long neat locs, and caramel skin. He opened the door for me and turned to pick me up. How he knew that my feet were swollen, and my body was close to shutting down, I don't have the slightest idea. Usually, his walk to the door was a straight shot, not once would he look back. Which wasn't like a gentleman; the lady should always be in front or beside a man, sheltered and farthest away from the street. I learned that from my hypocritical father who abandoned me at a very young age. Pleased that he cleaned up his act and began to use his manners, there was no way to hide the disconnection that was between us. Could the man that I just met a couple hours ago really have that much of a toll on me? Whatever the case may be, there was no way Dale was going to find out. *No way!* There was already too much going on between us that he wasn't even aware of. He didn't know about my late night searching for evidence, or my curiosity sparked by his actions. He thought that there was nothing wrong and that everything was going great. But like the Titanic, our ship was slowly sinking. Eventually, we would be broken in half and torn apart for good if no one tried to fix it. He was the type to ignore the elephant in the room instead of acknowledging its presence. If it were left up to him, we would crash and burn.

Personally, I had hope for us. I wasn't raised to just quit, and there was no way I would let him go without a fight. There were so many tears, so much hurt, and so much put into this relationship that we couldn't just let it all go to waste without trying to mend everything.

Being carried into the house for once was a great. It felt like he was trying to make things better. Unfortunately, it was offset by the feelings that were developing in my mind for Clayton. Why the hell were feelings already there for this man that was brand new to me? It was so far beyond my understanding that it kind of pissed me off. Ignoring all the possible reasons running through my mind, I snapped back into reality. On the dining room table there was a cake, one tier with white and red icing. Wow. I wonder why Dale was being so nice and thoughtful. Did I forget the day? Was it our anniversary? There were rose petals on the ground leading to the second floor of our condo. A couple tears started to stream down my face. As sincere as they were, I didn't know why they were there. Sweet tears then turned into salty whaling cries. For some reason, the emotional part of me came out, the part of myself that I never saw anymore. And with that came frustration. Why am I crying? Why can't I stop? Dale looked at me, kissed me, smiled, then put me down.

"Go unwind, I'll meet you downstairs when you're finished." He tapped my ass and walked into the kitchen, leaving me with a mind full of unanswered questions about why he was doing all of this. The curious heart was also for Clayton. There wasn't any reason why he should have been on my mind, especially at a time like this. I had a lot of thinking to do, and fast.

CHAPTER THREE

The sun woke me up the next day, no memory from the night before was left in my body. It seemed sort of like my soul was missing, like the air in my lungs was tampered with, and my heart was internally bleeding out. I hadn't looked over yet, but I knew that there was nobody but myself in the condo. Empty walls, empty space, but an overwhelmed and thirsty mind. There was a specific presence that was felt, a certain feeling. A feeling far from unfamiliar, but repetitively ignored.

—

As a child, my mother used to tell me to stay away from little boys. They had no good intentions with me, and all they wanted was sex. Although at our age, that may have very well been true, but implanting such a negative thought in a child's mind is nothing less than sinister. These are the thoughts that affect how us as women look at our men. These are the things that we speak into existence. All we are doing is making our young women bitter towards our young men based off our past situations. Not every man is sex driven, but believe me, if he isn't, it won't be long before he is. Not by nature, but by nurture. You learn culture, you learn racism, you learn to cook, you learn how to read, you learn how to write, you learn reactions, and you learn and develop preferences. Need I say more? So, all the while your daughter is growing up to be the independent bitter woman that you taught her to be. Someone else's son is growing up to be the reckless sex driven man that the world already assumes that he is. Every older black woman that I know told me the same thing growing up. My aunt, my grandmother, my mother's friends, the church ladies, and Sunday school teachers would all say the exact same thing. "These little boys don't want nothing but sex." They sounded like a broken record. Then they'd turn around and praise the little boys they were referring to.

We are all curious as children, and to be honest, I completely disagree that it's the little boys that are so sex driven. I have plenty of friends that initiated sex with their boyfriends out of curiosity. I was one of them. My mom talked about the shit so much and how bad it was that it made me want to do it. I was a true rebel at heart. Anything I was told not to do, I did it just because. Especially that.

—

When Dale does something sweet for me, he always follows up with something equally insulting. How do you make my night as perfect as it was and then be gone before the sun comes up? These are the things that prove to me that his mind is elsewhere. My inner thoughts reminded me how much of a hypocrite I am slowly becoming. Here I am pointing the finger, and I was just having all these vivid thoughts of a man that I only knew for a few hours. Memories of everything that happened the day before are gone, but I can still remember Clayton's face, his smell, the way he walks, and the goosebumps he gave me when he looked my way. I imagined him in the shower with me. Sex across the walls. I wanted to know what he felt like, and how he looked when intimate. I wanted to feel him kiss and touch my body.

It was in the shower where the guilt came. With every drop of water there was a thought of lust. It must have been an hour before my body became cold. Tears started to roll down my face. Why am I so upset? Then the frustration came. Ignoring the cold, I took the wash cloth and began to soap it up. Caressing my body, my mind went wild again. My thoughts are what drove me insane. My mind was fogged with ideal situations and layers of what the future held. There was no happiness inside of me. This man that I just met sparked so much of my interest that I began to question my current situation.

I wondered if people called him Clay. Does he have any kids? Does he like writing and intellect as much as I do? Does he like to people watch? Was he even interested? Does he have a relationship or situationship? Does he like movies? Does he drink? Maybe we could hang out sometime.

"Baby are you OK?"

Coming back to my senses I calmed myself down.

"Yes, just enjoying alone time."

Although his face wasn't visible behind the shower curtain, it wasn't hard to tell that he didn't believe a word that came out of my mouth.

"Noel, I'm stepping out for a while. I left you something on the table downstairs. See you when I get back. I love you."

"I love you too," I said, nonchalantly. He was full of bullshit. So, you leave before I awake and come back just to leave again? I took a deep breath. Suddenly my anger faded away.

—

Fully dressed, walking past the dining room made my mouth drop in awe. The curtains were open, sun was shining in on me, and I'm almost certain that if there was a magazine article about a woman being surprised by her significant other, I'd be the cover photo with a three-page article. Mouthing to myself, "Oh my God," I picked up a piece of paper that read,

"For my sweetest love, you deserve much more than a random act of kindness. I worship the ground you walk on. I know that I cannot give you the world, but I can give you a piece of me. I love you, Noel. See you when you get off."

Good lord, why are you doing this to me? Why when I find my man creeping, you send another man to my life that's just waiting to sweep me off my feet? You don't have to tell me, I can feel it. The signs are more than clear. Then at the same time, it's as if you told Dale about my suspicions, and now he's making a fool out of me. *Now* he decides to get his act together? Why, why, why?

There were keys to a brand-new off-white Tahoe on the table. To be honest, I didn't know Dale even listened to my nagging. These months of complaining about me not having a car paid off. It's not like I couldn't get a car myself, it's just that after the bad accident I got into three months ago that totaled my Accord, I started to really buckle down with work and school. This was my last year and there was nothing standing in my way of receiving my rightfully earned degree. So instead of picking up more hours with Tisa, I just saved my money and put my focus on school. A high car note wasn't attainable. My credit was still under construction and unfortunately, rent wasn't reported to any of the three credit bureaus.

I couldn't help but think, "touring in my Tahoe," to myself as I grabbed my keys and walked toward the cream painted truck. Having not smiled like this in a very long time, I'm positive this would have made the newest "bitter bitch" meme. I can see it now, a picture of me smiling with my keys in my hand standing right beside my new Tahoe with the caption, "Get you a man that listens and invests in your future. Stop fucking with those damn crazy niggas." Rolls eyes. The crazy thing about this is, the material things don't matter because Dale is still fucking around with Trinitee, I just can't prove it with actual evidence yet. So yeah, he's doing well as of now, but as soon as the evidence surfaces, he can have his keys and his ride, and cruise solo. I'll never play the fool, I don't care what you have to offer. But now isn't the time to voice that, so my mouth is shut until further notice.

CHAPTER FOUR

"You're glowing today. Tell me what the reason is. Who's the special guy?" he asked as he walked over to my desk. He had on a nice fitted suit that complimented his broad shoulders, and I couldn't help but to eye the bulge in his pants. Clayton was fishing for information, but if he wanted to play these lame elementary games, then I'd play right along. What he didn't know was that I wasn't one to play fair.

With a smirk, I bent over my desk and whispered, "You. You look nice in red." I licked my lips and immediately rolled my eyes. He just laughed.

"Oh yeah…You like that?"

"I'm pretty sure you have better things to do than be concerned about what or who for that matter is making me happy. Don't go looking for what you don't want to find, Mr. Davis. If you were attempting to ask me about my love life, I'll give you all the information you need, just come live and direct. I'm not one to play too many games. Yes, I'm with someone. And as much attention that you pay me, you've probably seen me getting in and out of my boyfriend's car. Any other questions? Or will that cease the interrogation?"

He just looked astonished. The smile that was spread across his face was now gone and he was painted with guilt and embarrassment. It was clear he was at a loss for words. And just as I felt bad for cutting him up the way I did, he turned and began to walk away saying something so faint I almost failed to hear him.

"I think you're beautiful, Ms. Gray."

I had to roll my eyes once more for that one.

"I apologize for offending you, but if I may add, no woman happy in her relationship would have been unbalanced and as on edge as you were just now. So, allow me a day with you to change your way of thinking." He turned back to me to see my facial expression, looking me dead in my eyes. "You don't have to act all of the time. I know your position. You do what you do well. But I sense that there is a softer side to you. The side that attracted me to you the first day that I saw you. Call me when you get uncomfortable at home." And with that, he walked back to his desk and began working on his assignments.

The look on my face was priceless. In more ways than one, I just lost this battle. He now knows that I'm interested and if my lack of a comeback didn't say it enough, my facial expression certainly did. He sees that my relationship is rocky, saw that all in my reaction, and now he practically knows that I'm considering his offer in taking me out.

Usually, women that are in love talk about their men all the time. I barely bring Dale up at work. The fact that I had no response just confirmed that I was interested in him. I couldn't deny it, so I didn't even try to perform damage control. Looking down at my computer, I saw a business card in the corner of my screen. Picking it up, the name Clayton Davis read in bright red ink. I didn't even think of reading the number on it. Oh no, he wasn't going to get me. Somewhere in my mind I kept hearing myself say, "Don't look up, do not look up, do not give this man the satisfaction." But ignoring that little voice in my head, I looked up and caught eyes with this mysterious man. I couldn't help but grin as we locked eyes and he gave me a wink. After a moment, I broke the glance, put his business card in my purse, and got back to the work I had in front of me.

"He's a very nice man, Noel." Tisa said with a little bit of sarcasm as she approached my desk. She knew exactly what she was doing. She hired this man for her own enjoyment. Her giving me a promotion was just as insincere as her offering him the job in my place. She could guess I'd be attracted to him but was aware of me having a man at home. It's like she always had to be evil. My pain and suffering seemed to be her way of happiness. She knew I was uncomfortable with my relationship and had to add fuel to the fire. Everything in me wanted to slap the shit out of her. But in these situations, I was taught to keep quiet.

Taking a deep breath, I responded, "Seems like I have some matchmaking to do." I winked at her, smiled, and got back to work.

This bitch has some nerve. If I could nominate her for most scandalous woman of the year, I swear I would without a second thought. But she was the one who deposited the checks in my account. She was in fact the one who could take my career to the next level, so it was best to play along. But at this point, she was fucking with my private life, convincing me that she had something up her sleeve. See, my mother told me about her type. True snakes. She acted like she wanted the best for me but in reality, she was continuously testing me and hoping I would fail. I was hip and believe me, she knew that the awareness was high. This was a part of the game that she played, so taking all of that into consideration, I made a game plan. She had to appear to come out on top without winning. Let the games begin!

—

As the weeks passed, I kept conversations with Clayton short. Besides the outside of the office talk we had to have, there was nothing left to say to him. Me letting him think he won that day was the icing on the cake. But to my surprise, he hadn't tried to come on to me since then. Tisa was also quiet, which was unusual. She even invited Dale and me to a party she was hosting in the hills. I politely declined though. It wasn't work related and smelled like trouble from a mile away. She never extended an offer to go anywhere with her before he came along, I wasn't going to risk it now. She was still plotting against me.

Although Dale bought me a Tahoe, nothing had changed. He was still absent, and I was still suspicious. The elephant remained in our bedroom. One morning while home alone, I found myself emptying my purse, coming across Clayton's business card in my wallet. A smirk spread wide across my face. I should call him. I waited a while to act on his offer, so I wasn't too thirsty. He told me to call when I was uncomfortable at home. Well, I was extremely uncomfortable. Dale only came home twice a week now, and I had no idea why. But I kept quiet. I wasn't going to leave so what's the point of arguing? I picked up my phone and dialed the number on the card.

"Hey Clayton, I was looking through my purse and thought I should call you. Hope you didn't have any plans today. I'm almost dressed so you should be prepared to pick me up in about half an hour. I'll send you the address once we hang up the phone. I look forward to seeing you outside of work."

I didn't give him a chance to answer, just hung up the phone and sent the text. Almost instantly, he replied with a winking emoji. Boom.

While applying my makeup, my mind went wild. I couldn't help but chuckle at myself for two reasons: One, I knew exactly what I was doing. First things first, this man thinks that I'm opening up to him, not only because of the call I made, but because I sent him my address to come get me. The same address that's shared with my man. He thinks there is established trust. And two, he thinks that I'm uncomfortable at home, which is true. But the situation was bearable. It's not like I was about to drop my whole relationship for him. I'm sure Tisa would get a kick out of this if she knew it was happening. See, I know I kind of bash her a lot and call her a snake from time to time, but I think she really does want the best for me. She just has a hard exterior. If she really wanted me to fail, then I wouldn't have been working for her for so long. Finding someone who wants an administrative job isn't that hard and I'm sure being able to work with one of the greatest in her field would fill the position before I could say, "I quit." She just tested me, and I hated it. But I will prevail, no matter what the challenge. I think she knew that and that's why she had no issue testing me all the time. But there were times when Tisa looked out for me. We've had heart to hearts and she advised me like a good mentor should. So, I can't really say she's all bad, I just don't know her motive all the time and it bothers me. It sends me off the edge and my anxiety gets the best of me, so I keep my eyes open. I don't trust her, but I don't trust anyone so it's nothing personal at all.

Last week I went shopping with my mother and bought a dark chocolate colored matte lipstick. This a special occasion, so I painted my lips with it and proceeded to the door. I dropped a note to Dale on the table saying that I'd be out with my mother until the morning. Swaying my hips, I locked the front door then waited for Clayton to open the passenger side of his ride. He kissed my hand and helped me in his low sitting all black Mustang. He closed the door gently and looked over at me to smile. This was the beginning of something beautiful.

CHAPTER FIVE

Everything in front of me was moving slow. Every beat of my heart felt as though the whole world could hear it. My stomach felt empty, but my liver was filled with liquid courage. Maintaining balance while staying caught up wasn't supposed to be so difficult, being that all of this was planned. But I was having too much fun in character.

We drove a few hours to a place called Hocking Hills. It was gorgeous. Gazing at the beautiful scenery and waterfalls made me want to come back in my spare time and bring one of my clients for a video shoot. Nearby there was a movie theatre and a small shopping center that contained a diner like restaurant. St. Anne Elizabeth's was the name. You'd think that this far up in Ohio there wouldn't really be too many restaurants. But man, the food was excellent to say the least. Clay ordered some type of pasta and light Alfredo sauce with smoked sausage and chicken. I don't mess with swine, so I kept it simple and just ordered a cheesy rigatoni dish. Even the simplest things can be jazzed up because that was the best rigatoni that I've tasted in a long time. It was served with a glass of Movendo. I'm not sure if he was stalking me and figured out that this was my favorite wine or what, but without my request, it was poured right in front of me, the bottle placed in the middle of the table.

"So how did you know Movendo was my favorite wine?" I asked him.

He laughed to himself. "I didn't but my sister loves it. I like bitter wines and brandy. I'm more of a champagne and D'Ussé type of guy. Most women like fruity, pretty shit."

I laughed with him.

"I love your smile. I think that's the best quality about you."

I looked down. I was nervous, and it showed.

"Am I making you uncomfortable? If I am, I'll stop."

I shook my head no. "Not at all, just a little nervous."

His head swerved back and to the side. "You? Nervous? I thought I'd never see the day."

I assured him that I was human just like him. His comment made me realize that I really had an issue with acting like I had no emotions. I acted so hard, like nothing bothered me. As if I felt no pain. It was an involuntary defense mechanism, and I wanted it to end. I had to let go of the memories that made me this way. And forgive myself to move on.

We laughed as we ate. It was entirely too sincere to be a part of my plan, but it worked. I wanted him to think we were hitting it off right, so that when we returned to work, I could be strictly about business. I wanted to toy with him and make him work for me. Since my boyfriend never put any effort toward keeping me, it felt good to be wanted. Not once did I think that I'd be nervous or that the flow wouldn't be right with this encounter, but I definitely didn't expect for this to come this naturally. I've never cheated on Dale, never even gave another man the time of day. Let's be honest, two wrongs don't make a right and the hypocrisy wasn't going to make anything better. Looking on the bright side, this was just a way of letting me know that I still had my "game" and was still a boss at heart. Everybody goes through things but being cheated on made me feel as though I lost my touch and I wasn't a catch anymore. But as they say, one man's trash is another man's treasure. So here I was, being another man's pot of gold and my man's throw away. The irony.

Clay asked me if I wanted to go back to the city or just stay where we were. To be completely honest, I was a bit intoxicated from the overindulgence of wine and a little blazed from the herbs we smoked a little earlier. I would have never guessed that he smoked. He seemed like a square guy. That's what I meant by mysterious, I knew it was something about him, but I couldn't put my finger on it. I thought I was going to turn him out, but he was putting me on to things I would have never assumed he was into.

If I was in the car for a drive longer than an hour, I was certain I would be asleep and my randevú wouldn't go as planned. I wasn't going to take that chance, so we both opted with staying put. Maybe more attention should've been paid because it was like he almost knew we would be staying there. A key magically appeared in his hand, and before I knew it, we had arrived at a cabin like home. He's a joke, this was beyond predictable, and it annoyed me in such a way that being discrete wasn't an option.

"Aren't you enjoying yourself?"

Damn I need to fix my face. Putting my index finger over my lip I mouthed "Shhhhh."

The lights were dim, I could see his silhouette but nothing more. He kept trying to talk, but finally realized it was time to be silent when I pushed him on the bed and started undressing as I walked toward the bathroom. Now fully naked, I ran the water over my hand and started the shower. I took my time and felt up my body, preparing myself for what was about to go down. I started to sing Beyoncé's "Speechless." I did it for my own enjoyment, but once I heard him say, "Damn, she can sing too?" I knew he was enjoying it just as much as I was.

My phone was on do not disturb. It was almost like he read my mind as I stepped out of the shower in my towel, the room started spinning and music automatically started to play. I was seriously a light weight, this was so embarrassing. All the sex songs we listened to as kids without our parent's permission were on a playlist. I walked over to the bed where Clayton was sitting in the same exact place I left him. I slowly pulled his legs apart and eased my body between them, dropping my towel behind me. Grabbing his manhood through his jeans, I looked him dead in his eyes. The room was still spinning, I was really drunk from the wine and blazed from the weed and didn't notice until this moment that he looked more than nervous.

"Relax. I thought this was what you wanted," I whispered, brushing my right hand on the side of his face, lifting off his manhood. "We can stop if you want."

He looked me in my eyes then looked down at my hand resting on him. He leaned closer and kissed my forehead, then my cheek, and over to my lips. One peck on my lips, then he pulled back. Another peck and he pulled back again. Three pecks and once more, he pulled his head back and away, leaving me eager to touch them again. I leaned forward, letting my breast sway and took a kiss from him. He leaned back again in the middle of me trying to caress his tongue with mine. The more he withdrew the more I wanted to kiss him. We played this game until my entire body was on top of his and the small pecks turned into a drawn-out kissing contest. I was so aggressive, I was embarrassed because he slowed me down and kissed me with passion. I can tell he was thrown off at the way I advanced.

"Relax, " he whispered as he showed me how to do things the correct way.

Usually, during my first sexual encounter with someone, I take control. That is exactly what I thought I was about to do after I somehow got him out of his clothes. Wrong again, Noel. He gracefully flipped my body over so fast, like a master chef in a pancake tournament. He didn't have to open my legs, they spread apart instantly. Clayton was obviously in shape. He wasn't the total opposite of skinny, but he wasn't an athlete either. I honestly admired it, way more than I admired Dale's muscular frame. It gave me a sense of security, a sudden rush of excitement.

"I don't want to stop," he whispered. My confusion was redirected to pleasure when he began kissing my pussy lips up to my clit. Deep breath, Noel. I tried so hard to not give him all the satisfaction, but with every stroke of his tongue, a burst of pleasure shot through my body. I found myself trying not to call out and taking tremendously big breaths in and out, in and out, until I could no longer keep quiet.

"*Shit!*"

He looked up and smiled at me and at that moment, I was ready. The liquid courage did play a huge part in bringing out my wild side, there's no denying that. And usually I wouldn't be able to get down like this with a man I wasn't familiar with mentally, but he intrigued me. The more I looked at him, the wilder I became. By this time, my heart was beating outside of my chest. I'm pretty sure that he heard it. Shit, I'm sure the cabin to the left of us heard it. But I didn't want it to stop.

I decided to go down and return the favor. Every slurp got louder and the suction of my lips gripping his dick got tighter. My mouth grew wetter and the sloppier I became the more his dick grew. Abruptly, he stopped me, and I didn't miss my chance to get on top. I rode him like my life depended on it and honestly, I'm not even that good at riding! I didn't want to stop. There was cream everywhere and I was too drunk to even pay attention to his facial expressions. In my mind, he felt better in me then I felt on him. He pushed himself deeper and deeper inside me and started shifting my body over until he ended up on top of me. Closing my eyes, I submitted my body to him, giving him all control. All I remember was my little flower creating a whirlpool, Twista's "Wetta" playing in the background, my body shifting from his stroke, and firm grip on my sides. It was over. His body collapsed onto mine, his strokes slowed down, our heart beats increased, and I saw fireworks. The room went black and there was silence. I was satisfied. This was the night I gave him a piece to my puzzle, it was up to him to put everything together. In the morning, I found out he knew more about me than I initially believed.

CHAPTER SIX

"You like to be in control," Clayton said as the sunlight hit his cheeks. He looked so good.

"Are you asking or telling me?"

He smirked. "Telling. It's cute."

I laughed, "Cute!? I'm a grown ass woman. Ain't shit about what I do 'cute.' Besides, That's not true. I like a challenge."

He placed his right hand on my thigh and began to rub it. "Yeah alright. You want to know what I like about you?"

I looked up from my phone. I was checking to make sure Dale didn't call or text. He didn't. I tried to brush it off, but it pissed me off the more I thought about it. I tried to give Clayton my attention, but by this time it was written all over my face.

"You're dedicated."

This comment intrigued me. I put my phone face down on my lap and thought for a few seconds before I responded.

"You barely know me. For all you know, I could just be doing the bare minimum and getting by. That was random, where did that even come from?" He had my full attention now.

"I see good qualities in people and I address them. You're sincere with everything you do. You're genuine and you work hard. I watch you sometimes at work. You're focused. You have a good head on your shoulders for 23. When I was that age, I was focused, but not like you. I can tell you are serious about your career."

I nodded and went silent. I was nervous again. He was always so calm, quiet, and well mannered. That made me so nervous and interested at the same time. My phone rang, it was my mother. I answered and told her that I'd call her back later. I leaned over and turned the volume up on the radio. I didn't want to talk anymore. I kept checking my phone to see if Dale called, but there was no luck.

For the rest of the ride home, Clayton kept asking me if I was alright. My response was a quick, "Yes." He could sense that I was bothered so I reassured him that it wasn't because of him. At that moment, I think he realized that it was my boyfriend. What I liked about Clayton was that he never mentioned Dale and never said anything about me being in a relationship while I was with him. He simply didn't bring it up, which was great because I didn't want to talk about it at all. I just wanted my time with him to be my time with him and he let it be just that. I respected that. He dropped me off and kissed me goodbye. I usually don't kiss, but I was fond of Clayton, so I enjoyed the peck and kept it moving. There was silence after our kiss, but I'm positive he could sense that I had a strong liking for him already. All that meant was I'd have to ignore him for a while. The key was to not sweat him. Even though I wanted to see him again outside of the office, I wouldn't act on it, even if asked.

Instead of coming home to an angry boyfriend, I came home to an empty condo. Not much of a surprise, but the fact that there was no call, text, or facetime sent to my phone was complete and total bullshit. The night before was amazing, there was no denying that. But why didn't my boyfriend text to check on me? This was unusual. Dale stayed out late most nights, but he almost always sent a text to let me know that he's been at work late, even though I knew it was a lie. Last night I got nothing: no call, no text, no email, nothing, and I was pissed. The whole point of going out with Clayton was to have Dale up and worried about me like I do him. But that plan wasn't successful.

Once inside, I began pacing around the kitchen where I noticed the cabinet under the sink was slightly open. I reached down to close it and something red caught my eye. Well, well, well, there it is! I just couldn't help but to laugh at the fact that there were red lace panties on my kitchen floor. This had to be a fucking joke. I'm sure that if someone were watching me, they would think that I was out of my mind. I began to laugh hysterically as if someone told me a seriously funny joke. My blood pressure shot up as rage took over my body. My blood was boiling and as corny as it may sound, I'm certain that if you put an egg on my forehead, that motherfucker would fry! OK, that was a nice shot to the chest. But I wasn't satisfied, I wanted more.

Taking my precious time up the stairs, my mind froze. Now usually there would be a lot on my mind in an event like this, but unfortunately for Dale, my mind went blank. He was in fact the biggest dumbass in life. Instead of moving on, I kept egging the situation on. Let's take a look in the bathroom trash can. Rummaging around in the can, clearly disregarding how unsanitary my actions were, I found exactly what I was looking for. The golden ticket. That was all I needed to see. I dropped the panties and the condom wrapper in the middle of the floor and ran into my room. I took off like I was on the track team. I didn't make a mess. There was no bleaching of clothes, no fires started, I mean hey I live here too.

My hands were shaking and the air around me made me nauseous. I packed an overnight bag and ran down the stairs grabbing my keys, slamming the front door and the car door behind me as I got inside. There was dead silence in the car while I drove around trying to decide if I was going to a hotel, or if I was going to call Clay. No, not Clay. This was too fresh and bringing these types of problems to our situation would only make things worse and make me completely vulnerable. I mean, I was giving this nigga nicknames already. That's a definite no. OK so to the hotel it is. I pulled over to the nearest gas station and grabbed Dale's credit card. As I swiped the card and keyed our zip code in, I couldn't help but notice that I was still shaking terribly. I wanted to call him and tell him that I found his remains from what happened while I was gone, but that would give him the leeway to lie. Nah, if he decided to deny what was clearly in my face, I wanted to be there, so I could slap the shit out of him for disrespecting me a second time.

I got back in the car after pumping the gas and pulled out my phone. Hmmm, which hotel should I stay in tonight? Usually the Residence Inn would have been my first choice, but it was time for a change. My mind that was previously blank was now filled with an overabundance of questions. But the questions were for me, not him. I was disappointed in myself for continuously putting up with him. When I was a young girl, I would shake my head while watching my mother go through the same shit transpiring in my life at this very moment. It made me feel angry, shameful, and nauseous from disgust. My mother and I were not the same. She was married and dealt with the bullshit of her husband. My struggles with men in comparison were similar, but very immature and less extreme than what she endured. Either way, she wasn't anyone I wanted to be anything like.

—

I checked into the Courtyard by Marriott in Blue Ash. I rode past it daily on my way to work and never even noticed it. A nice tucked off building that had tan hues and screamed peace. I'm pretty sure that the car behind me may have been irritated by my driving. I was still shaking, and I needed to relax and calm down asap. I pulled into the hotel entrance and parked my car. I was so stressed out that I could barely walk straight. I stumbled into the hotel lobby and waited at the desk until someone came out to greet me. They must have been busy because I stood there for about five minutes before a middle-aged Indian man sped past the desk, telling me he'd be right with me. The lobby was empty, just like my heart. I just waited. I had no energy to go to another destination. Suddenly, a handsome bartender came around the back while the concierge checked me in yelling, *"Cousinnnnn!"* I was so confused at first until he continued to talk.

"If I knew you were going to be staying here, I would have booked for you so you could use my discount." He said looking directly at me. I caught on quickly.

"I didn't even know you worked here! It's been so long since I've seen you. You look so good! How have you been?" I was being careful not to go into too much detail and blow my cover. I really didn't even care about the cost of the hotel because all of this was being charged to Dale's Capital One card. He didn't know that though and I appreciated the gesture, so I went along with it. Once I was checked in, he told me that I could come down to the bar for some drinks on the house. I didn't have to work or go to class the next day and by the way things were going in my love life, I could say that I deserved a drink or two. So, after I checked into my room I got in the shower. This shower, like many others I've taken recently, was way longer than usual. I sat on the shower floor and let the water make its way down my body. There was a warm eerie feeling in my chest, it was indescribable. I longed to cry, I wish I could have just broken down and felt better afterward, but nothing came out. Is this my karma? Honestly, there wasn't a thing that I've done in my past that made me deserve this. Nothing! Sitting there in the dark and completely mind boggled, I got up and finally decided to wash the soap off my body and head to the bar.

When I got there, no one was there, not even the bartender. It was quiet throughout the halls, as if I wasn't supposed to be there. A weird feeling took over me and just as I got up to leave, the bartender came around the corner.

"I didn't think you were coming back. Sit down, relax, and stay a while. What you are feeling like tonight?"

I sat back down and gave him a forced smile. "Start me off with something light, it's been a long day. I can go for some Goose, something fruity."

"I can do that for you." He was quiet, handsome, big around the shoulders, nicely groomed, and tall. He caught drift of me checking him out and chuckled a little. "You don't look so bad yourself."

As brown as I was, my face turned red. I was really slipping lately when it came to men. This was not the first impression that I wanted to give him. Vulnerable and open, this nigga could read me like a book.

"I'm Noel. I didn't catch your name." I looked down at his badge. Jonathan was printed boldly. Fuck! I am really losing right now.

He just smiled while preparing my drink. "It's OK to be nervous. Relax, I'm not here to judge. I know you said you had a long day; do you want to talk about it?"

He placed my drink on the bar's coaster. I picked it up and took a sip. It was tasty and light, he knew how to follow directions. Now I usually wouldn't just tell my business, especially to another man, but the bar was empty, and we were the only ones in the lobby so fuck it, why not? I sipped my drink a few more times before responding. I had to watch him closely, he knew what he was doing. He made it clear that he was attracted, but he wasn't too thirsty. He let me sweat him. He knew I was vulnerable. He didn't tell me how beautiful I was like any other guy would right off rip. And even though he probably knew I was having trouble with men, he didn't mention it, not even a bit of reverse psychology. He let me tell him what I wanted him to know. I respected it, but it instantly had me on my toes.

"You ever feel like you just need a break from everything? I don't know, like you're going to explode if you don't take the chance to unwind? That's me right now. I'm all over the place. I have an ideal life and most people would kill to live like me at my age. My boyfriend pays my bills, I'm a full-time student, and I intern with one of the best film producers. I want for nothing."

"If I may ask, how old are you?"

I laughed and put my empty glass on the bar. "23, I'll be 24 in December."

His eyebrows lifted in disbelief as he went to make me another drink.

"You are the bartender make whatever you like, just nothing dark please. That is my only request. By the way, thank you for the drinks, I really appreciate this."

He smiled at me and looked me deep in the eyes. "It's my pleasure. You seem really mature for 23. It's all about energy with me. As soon as I saw you, I felt your energy and fell in love with it. I know that's corny and you probably hear shit like that all the time but it's sincere. Your vibe caught my attention, and I wanted to learn more about you. I see that you're upset, but I want to take your mind off that. You're way too pretty to be all upset like this. No disrespect to your man."

At this point, he had already put my second drink down and had his fingers on my chin. I'm a lightweight so I was already feeling it. I'm no dummy, I knew he was all game, but in this moment, I didn't care one bit and I was eating it up.

Over the past week, I really have gotten beside myself. I cheated once and damn near was about to cheat again. I know two wrongs don't make a right and yet, here I was entertaining this man. Every drink made me warm on the inside. My cookie was wet and throbbing. The more we talked, the more the fire inside me grew. I longed for everything that I wasn't receiving at home: attention, understanding, and love. Even if it was temporary. I wanted him, just for the night.

He began to look even more delicious with every sip. My world was spinning at this point as he was talking and showing off his white teeth. Lord knows what he was saying. I just interrupted him, I'm sure he didn't mind.

"What time are you off the clock?" I began to get up.

"I was off an hour and a half ago." We both started to laugh.

"Is it OK if I get in the Jacuzzi?"

He looked around. "I don't see why not."

At this point, I was drunk, so I leaned in and whispered that I wanted him to tag along. He explained that it was a conflict of interest, but I was demanding, so he finally agreed. He told me to go get changed and he'd meet me there. I brought a two-piece bikini and a one-piece that showed a lot of rear end. I wanted to create an illusion but still be tempting. I admired my curves in the one piece as I grabbed a towel and headed down the hall.

He was in the hot tub waiting for me and boy was he fine. He looked like a piece of white chocolate waiting to melt in my mouth. Usually, I'm not the biggest fan of lighter men, but he was everything I needed. My towel dropped gracefully, showing off my thick thighs and full breasts. His shoulders were still broad, even without a shirt. He had no chest hair, clear skin, and the hot bubbling water made the scene more tempting.

"Is all of that your real hair?"

I looked around and placed my hand on my hair. I had it in a bun, natural as it had been for years, with my baby hair laying gracefully. Nothing forced.

"Didn't your mother tell you to never ask a woman if her hair was real?" I chuckled. "Yes, this is all of my *real* hair. It took me all my life to grow it. So many memories and emotions are wrapped up in these follicles. Sometimes I want to cut it all off and start over. But of course, as a woman my insecurities bring me right back to just leaving it alone."

He nodded and just stared at me. It seemed like he wanted to respond more seriously but didn't know if he should go there, either because it would offend me, or because he knew I was drunk. I looked at him suddenly and asked what the look was for.

"Nothing," he said. "I just can see that you're battling yourself in some way." I began to ask what he meant but he cut me off. "Something internal is bothering you. Internal conflict is common, but I'm curious as to why a woman like you is having so much trouble overcoming it?"

I sat in thought for a moment and gave a fake smile and chuckle. He caught me slipping. I mean, initially my idea of this was just fucking and calling it a night. I thought we would get groovy and he'd disappear. This man was picking my brain and trying to get to know me. It bothered the hell out of me because a woman like me was usually on her toes, but I kept getting caught up. This was repetitively happening to me and it didn't sit well at all. He kept a blank stare, I couldn't read him. At that very moment I had to remind myself that I was very drunk and chilling out would help the situation more. I was going against the grain and thinking too hard. I just repetitively told myself in my head to relax and let everything be natural with him because in a sense, I was only upsetting myself.

"Let's play a game, if you're up to it." I said and moved away from him in the hot tub.

"Layout the rules," he said eagerly.

I took a deep breath and closed my eyes. "I guess I should have asked if you liked poetry before proposing this game. Do you? Like poetry?"

There was nothing but silence, so I opened my eyes to see him nodding his head yes.

"OK, good. So, you seem really interested in what's going on with me. So here is your chance to learn. Basically, what's going to happen is some freestyling. Sort of like rapping but in poetry form. I used to write poetry myself, I was just never bold enough to recite them to anyone. That's beside the point, OK… so I'm going to start off with a bar of poetry or whatever my heart desires. Whether it is a bar or two or three, I'll say it out loud. This is all freestyle. And then you'll do the same thing, but it'll relate to the same things. If you get what I'm saying."

He stopped me before I could finish. "Yes, I understand. This shall be interesting." He moved further in the corner where the jets were blasting and sat lower, so they were against his back.

"Everything will be kept confidential. Just give me a sec and I'll begin."

There was silence. I watched him close his eyes and I shut mine again. I sat lower in the hot water and embraced the steam hitting my face. The pool room was silent; all I could hear were the jets and some water from the ceiling dripping to the ground. Something I didn't hear until now. Everything was listening: Jonathan, the water, and all my surroundings. They were all in deep thought with open ears. When my mouth opened, my stomach fluttered because I had never heard any of this pain before. I had locked it up and lost it, hoping to never find it again. This was a side of me that I didn't even know or tap into yet. Surprising even myself, I finally spoke.

"I used to cry over spilled milk, and then I realized that the white slime was nothing but a bed of lies. I picked up almonds and mashed them with strawberries just to smear the paste over my third eye. It was sweet, it was lucid. It got me high and made me feel stupid. It made me think that I wasn't lonely, in a body with broken bones. With a dismayed spirit and a key to the most abandoned and broken home." I stopped suddenly and felt tears roll down my face. I was unsure if I was going to continue or not, but before I could open my mouth, he began to speak. My ears were open, just as my heart and my spirit. It was almost like he was singing to me.

"When you tried to open the door, was it locked? Was it gated? When the door finally opened, did the butterflies escape it? Leaving islands and islands of diamonds covered in your blood? Filled with sacrifices and sought out in your love. Did you touch it like I did? And realize that you aren't helpless. That you're selfless and more personable than reckless. Your song, I've sang in many more ways than one. It's the battle of your mind that you must learn to overcome. I mean, you're beautiful, and bold, light and quiet like the snow. But so cold I can't help but wonder when you'll ever let it go." He stopped and opened his eyes to me staring him down in tears. "You were supposed to keep your eyes closed."

We both laughed, until I tasted salt on my tongue. He came closer to me and gave me a hug. "It's going to be OK, I promise it will. I don't know you that well, but I see a lot of myself in you. You're going to look back on this and remember the thirsty bartender told me I was going to be alright." We laughed again, then I took his hand and led him back to my room.

—

We didn't have sex. We just shared intimacy, all night. And for once, I felt at peace. I didn't have to tell him everything that was going on with me internally for him to know. He didn't ask many questions, just saw that I was distraught and spoke on his observations. We had an understanding without a full conversation. That was simply amazing to me. But when I awoke, he was gone. A note on the bed said, "Don't forget how much you have to offer. - *Jonathan*." I sat up on the bed stale faced because he didn't leave a number for me to call. I wasn't finished with him. I was interested in this man. I was appalled and hurt. My heart sank into my stomach as if I was in love and he was just killed or something. The worst part is that I had no idea why I felt so strongly about this man already. In my times of need, I wanted to be able to have access to him. The night we shared was priceless. I've never experienced that with a man before and it was all gone just like that. It wasn't fair.

How could he just share such a sincere time in my life with me, and then leave with no explanation or contact? I guess he didn't owe me one. He didn't have to talk to me ever again. Chances are, we'd never see each other again and to be honest, if we did, I'm not certain I would even speak to him based off this alone. It was a cold thing for him to do. He knew how I was feeling, but he decided to not feed my wants or needs. He forced me to take care of them myself, even though I didn't want to. He taught me something, and even though I was hurt, ultimately, I respected him for it.

CHAPTER SEVEN

This was the morning after. I was supposed to feel like shit, but I didn't. Well, I did, but this was a different type of shit. I was supposed to be hungover but instead, I was love drunk. I was really losing my spunk. First, I fell for the okie doke with Clay, and now this mystery man that worked at the Courtyard by Marriott tapped into my mental. Honestly, what are the odds that during a week I would become vulnerable and let two different guys in? Not sexually, but mentally and emotionally. I hate to say it, but once I read that note that Jonathan left for me without a phone number, I was a little heart broken. For him, I wasn't worth his time and effort after our night together. I was so damn thirsty, it really zoned me out. I wanted to go downstairs and see if he worked later so I could possibly get his number. I was more than willing to come back up here and stalk him. The way that he made me feel was indescribable. I've never in all my years of living felt so wanted by any man. He made me feel like I was his top priority two hours into meeting him. He was so curious and seemed so genuine. I'm so used to being showered with gifts to cover up the bullshit transpiring right in front of my face. I was starting to be a spitting image of my mother and the thought of that just made me cringe. I felt sick. I wanted to throw up. That did way more damage than a hangover could ever do.

—

Checking my phone, all I saw were two missed calls from Clay with a follow up message saying that he was just checking my pulse, and a text from Tisa thanking me for working so closely with Clayton, followed by an invite to a dinner party she was attending tomorrow evening.

The semester was over, my boyfriend was obviously out cheating on me, and I was an emotional wreck. It made plenty of sense for me to go to this dinner party and have some fun. I accepted the invite and asked her what the attire was. I wasn't going to respond to Clay, I'd eventually see him at work. I didn't want him to think he was in control. Something was missing though. There was emptiness in my stomach. I realized that Dale still hadn't contacted me. I began to worry. Even though I did see the panties and the used condom, my thoughts went elsewhere. This really wasn't like him. So, I dialed his number and waited to see if he'd answer. Four rings and his voicemail. It rang for 30 seconds so that means he didn't forward my call. Hanging up, I decided that I should text him. Just a simple "call me" should do. Now all I had to do was wait on the call. That's when I realized that check out was in 10 minutes. I didn't have time to shower or freshen up, so I just grabbed my clothes from the previous night, stuffed them in my overnight bag, and brushed my teeth. I could do the rest at home.

Before leaving the king suite, I checked my phone one last time to see if there were any messages from Dale. Not one call, text, facetime, Insta DM, Facebook message, or anything. I hit the Instagram icon on my phone, opening the app and switched from my notifications to my follower activities. At first there was nothing, just some followers that I didn't even know why I was following liking random pictures and thirst traps. A few more scrolls down, I stumbled upon what I was looking for; Dale's active account liking someone's baby picture. Something told me right there to stop, and honestly, this time I should have listened to my intuition. Unfortunately for him, I clicked on the picture, read the caption, and almost passed out. There was a brown skinned newborn baby girl in the arms of a fair skin, long haired young woman that I had never seen before.

The caption read, "May 26th, 2016, Journey Paige stepped into our lives and changed it forever. She has her daddy's smile, a smile that could light up a room. This feeling I have holding you can't be put into words …"

I couldn't even read the rest. I tapped the picture lightly and saw that Dale was tagged in it. Scrolled down past all the congratulations and saw that he put a heart emoji underneath followed by, "Daddy's girl." I literally almost threw up at the thought. I could have stopped there but I went further, rowing myself down the pond of sorrow. I saw all their pictures: the picture of him holding their baby, the maternity pictures, and the couple's pictures. This left me in complete awe. How could I have not seen this? I was so wrapped up in him cheating with Trinitee that I didn't even predict that he had a whole other bitch pregnant. For nine whole months, I suspected nothing. I was sick, my body ached, and tears fell from my eyes. I locked my phone and walked to the elevator, took it down to the first floor, and walked out to the new Tahoe that Dale had bought me. I calmly packed my things in the trunk and drove off.

At this moment, I didn't know how to react. Everything was numb. I almost didn't feel the rain dripping on my skin from the windows being let down. I was hot, and I needed some air. My top priority was to stay focused enough to get home without crashing and killing myself or someone else. To be honest, I don't even know how I got home. I don't remember the ride, turning at any intersections, stopping at the stop sign right before I hit my street, or even pulling into the driveway. There was no memory of me getting out of the car.

It's almost like I floated into the house. I walked straight to my room to sit my bag down, past the flowers on the dining room table, and past Dale sleeping on the couch. I didn't even hear him say my name. I didn't hear him ask what was wrong. I just kept walking and once I reached the bathroom, I opened the toilet seat and threw up everything I consumed in the past week. I was so happy to release the toxins built up inside me. I didn't even realize that he was behind me, holding my hair. I didn't hear him ask me again what was wrong. I saw red. I looked him in the eyes and saw nothing. All the respect and love that I've ever had for this man was now gone. I'm certain he saw the pain and tears building up in my eyes. He wiped my face. I stepped back, telling him not to touch me, and walked into our bedroom. He was on my heels, asking what was wrong, and where I'd been, telling me he hadn't called because he planned this huge surprise and that my mother and other family members were waiting on us at some fucking restaurant.

I replied calmly, "Seems like they'll miss us today, I'm not going. As a matter of fact, I'm not going anywhere with you. I don't even want to breathe your air right now. If you were smart you'd move out of my way."

He moved as I tilted my head, watching him realize I was serious.

"Babe what's up? Why are you acting like this?"

I stopped and looked at him long and hard, I wanted to curse him out. Hell, I wanted to beat his ass. But instead, I continued to pack my bag, keeping my back turned to him.

"Just two days ago, I was in love with you. It pained me to be on a mini vacation with another man. Every kiss he gave me, and every ounce of affection made me feel guilty because even though you aren't perfect by any means, I thought I had a good man waiting on me at home. And when we made love, it hurt me that I was falling out of love with you."

I turned to him and looked him in the eyes, trying to fight the tears.

"Then, I came home and found a condom wrapper, some red lace panties that were too damn big to even question if they were mine, and an empty house. Even after you didn't contact me, even after the bartender at the hotel last night made me feel like the luckiest woman in the world, I was still angry with myself for not doing right by you."

I reached for my purse and grabbed his credit card, calming myself, because at this point I was yelling.

"Oh, here's this." I said as I gave him his credit card back.

He just stared at me, straight faced. The room was silent and felt gloomy from the rain outside and the mood of the current situation.

"I questioned myself and now here I am looking you dead in the eye and I see nothing. You're nothing to me. You're disgusting. Filthy and worthless."

He said nothing. I mean what could he really say? He just stared at me, his eyes were low and glossy.

"Congratulations, on your new baby girl. I guess I wasn't lucky enough to meet her." I turned my back on him once more. There was a longer period of silence, which made me turn to see if he was still in the room. There he was looking pitiful, head down staring at his feet. I just shook my head and continued what I was doing.

"I'm sorry," he almost whispered and walked out of the room. Waiting until he left, I slid to the floor and balled up. The sobbing was continuous but there were no more tears. I heard him open and close the door behind him on his way out and at the very moment, I suddenly felt like the lowest creature on earth. I just laid there on the carpet looking out the window at the dark clouds, listening to the rain beat on the roof. I didn't feel like a business professional, I didn't feel pretty, I didn't feel like I was a catch at that point. I tried to make myself believe that I was a gem and that any man was lucky to have me, but obviously that wasn't the case. There were no more games being played because ultimately, I lost a long time ago. I wanted this to be a dream, I wanted it to be a joke, I wanted to wake up and this be a figment of my sick wicked imagination. So, I went to sleep in hopes of a better reality when I woke.

Was this my karma? If I hadn't gone up the road with Clayton, if I had not cheated, if I would have just waited at home for Dale to return, would he still have a child with someone else? If I didn't find the Instagram of the other woman, would he have been here waiting for me? Would the child not be here? Or was I destined to cross this path in my life anyway? I couldn't help but think that this was all my fault. If I wouldn't have been sneaking around. If I wasn't snooping I would have never found the picture of the baby girl and she wouldn't have existed. Either that or I just would have been blind to her existence. Would he have told me? I doubt it. Would he still be acting like nothing was wrong? Who the fuck was he fucking? If she just had a baby, I'm positive that he wasn't fucking her in any lace panties here in our home. I was stupid. I was useless. I was oblivious to the things happening in my life. I wanted to die. I was humiliated, embarrassed, and hurt. It was way too much to bear. I was overwhelmed and couldn't help but feel sorry for that little girl. Her father lived two completely different lives. I know it didn't matter now but it would when she grew up and questioned him as a man. She'd eventually learn his deepest and darkest secrets. She'd be ashamed and hurt because her father hurt another innocent woman by creating her. It'll hurt her, confuse her, and have her looking at her father as less of a man. She'll be angry like I was with my father and turn her nose up at him. And he'll weep and be so sorry. But it'll never be enough to change the image that she would have in her head for him. Sad, the black American dad story. Crazy right?

CHAPTER EIGHT

The sun woke me the next day, bright and early. I didn't have to go look to see that the house was empty; there was a feeling of emptiness inside me. I was curled up in the middle of the floor, with the sun shining in on me. Reaching up on the bed I found my phone, it was dead, and I didn't have the slightest idea of what time or day it was. Assuming a day had passed while I was sleeping, I got up and walked around, plugging my phone up to the charger. The door was unlocked. Dale probably didn't lock it when he left yesterday. The area that we lived in wasn't one to worry about though, so I really wasn't concerned. Plus, we had an alarm system, so if the door was opened I'd hear the alarm go off.

Walking into the kitchen, I looked at the time on the stove. 3:15?! I have to get ready! Tisa was expecting me at the office at 6:00 so we could ride to this dinner party together. Showering, painting my face with makeup, and putting my thick hair up would take at least two hours. There was a fluttering in my stomach and I had no idea why. But for some reason it was hard to shake it. I don't usually get nervous for events like this. I mean, it was just a dinner party. Maybe the fluttering was due to the events that had been transpiring in my life lately. Maybe I was afraid to get back out there again. Personally, I believe it was 50/50, both of those reasons were the cause. It made me uncomfortable and I wanted it to stop, immediately.

—

I arrived at the office with 15 minutes to spare. Tisa hadn't pulled up yet, so I sat in my car and listened to music. I decided to paint my body in my favorite red dress. It was solid red, mid-length with short sleeves, and hugged my hips while showing the right amount of cleavage. It made me feel like me again. This past week I lost myself, and it was time to get back to me. I wasn't the type to sit around and pity myself for days at a time. I wanted to get back out there as soon as possible. I know my emotions weren't going to disappear into thin air, but this would help more than crying all day long and feeling sorry for myself. Although I was sure I'd receive some attention, that wasn't my goal. My goal was selfish and all about me. It was to get back in the rhythm of openly being me. My hair was blown out and curled tight. I lightly beat my face just to add a little glow. I was beautiful, this was something I was sure of, but sometimes forgot because of the daily load that I took on. My heart and mind were heavy, but I was willing to go out and at least attempt to have a good time.

Tisa pulled up in a white Tesla and honked her horn. Every time I felt she was just an ordinary person with an ordinary life, I was reminded that she lived well below her means. She was humble, but that girl has money. She secured the bag very early and was confident in who she was and where she was going. Even when I disliked her, I still held the utmost respect for her because of her branding and the way that she carried herself. She was generally a private person, with the right amount of class. She did it all by herself and she took pride in that, enough to make a man proud but in a humble enough way that she didn't intimidate her prey. She was fierce to say the least. I wanted to talk to her and get some advice, but I didn't have the courage to open up to her about my personal life. She was 42, a bit older than me and way more established. Initially I thought it would be a great idea because I looked to her as a mentor, but the more I thought about it, the more I saw it as a conflict of interest. She was my boss at the end of the day, and too much of a mix of business and personal was never good. I learned that from her.

"Are you OK?" She asked calmly as I lowered myself into her vehicle. I didn't even notice the deep thought written all over my face.

"Yes, I am just a bit nervous," I said, reassuring myself more than reassuring her. She didn't respond, she just turned her music up a bit louder. She was quiet and difficult to read at times. That was something that I both admired and hated.

"You look great! Maybe you'll find a new man tonight." She said jokingly. She would never encourage me to look for a mate at a business outing.

I smiled and thanked her. "You look stunning as well! As you always do."

She smiled, showing all her teeth which meant she really appreciated my compliment. I sized her up because for some reason, tonight, she looked as if she was glowing. She was in a white silk dress that complimented her legs. Her light tan skin looked like butterscotch, as if she was dipped in butter. And her hair, naturally straight, was styled with a middle part in the front, and flowed down her back. She was stunning! Her faint freckles were evenly spread across her face and her baby hairs laid on her hairline. Her gold choker complimented her skin and her breasts sat up perky and small. She was slim with the right amount of weight in all areas. She ate healthy and stayed active while balancing her job and personal life. She did it so effortlessly, with the help of me of course. Well Clayton now, my personal assistant days were over, and man was I happy about that. I now performed in person consultations with clients, handled the email list and any communication that Tisa needed to have with current or future clients. In our office, communication was key. Tisa, Clayton, and I communicated to each other in regard to her schedule and dealings. She was a creative director and set organizer for films. She wasn't cheap, but she always delivered and because of that, her business was expanding rapidly. She didn't go out often but when she did, it was always with a purpose. She was well respected and coming up in the industry. She now was focusing on publicity and putting a face to her name, so of course when she went out to these types of events, she put on her Sunday's best. She always kept it simple and remained confident.

Although my focus wasn't directing, being able to work closely with her contributed to my career. I was more focused on screenwriting. Screenwriting, directing, camera work, and editing pretty much all go hand in hand. Working with her opened doors to networking and there was a possibility of her expanding and eventually collaborating with me. I was gaining the first-hand experience that I needed. I was blessed to be in the situation that I was in, even at times when I became ungrateful and impatient. Lately I've been forgetting that I had more access than any regular film student. Her client base was amazing, and I dealt with them all first hand. I had to remind myself that I certainly was in a position many people hoped for but never were lucky enough to get. I've never really been around her outside of work, this was a different side of Tisa I haven't really seen. The sweet, genuine caring Tisa. The usual envious, sarcastic remarks didn't happen, but I was prepared for it.

We pulled up to a nice house in Amberley Village, with a long driveway that was filled with Escalades, BMWs, Rolls Royces, Bentleys, and Aston Martins. There was a man dressed in an all-white suit standing near the pathway that led to the back patio, crossing off names on the list. When we got closer, Tisa told him our names and he opened the gate for us to walk through. Almost instantly, she was greeted by rich bougie normal looking people with high ranks in the film industry. She was calm, sweet and polite, and introduced me every time she greeted someone new. I'm not going to lie, I was overwhelmed. I was friendly but being at an event like this with so many people that held weight in the industry made me nervous. I was more observant than social, and it wasn't a secret.

"You look amazing tonight," I heard a distant and familiar voice say from behind me. I turned to see Clayton's face. He was dressed in a nice all black suit and white tie.

"You don't look so bad yourself," I chuckled. He gave me a hug and whispered in my ear to relax. My unease was written all over my face, and he was encouraging me to use the charm that we both knew I had. I smiled as he let me go and winked at me, walking in the opposite direction. He was so damn fine! But it was just something about him that I couldn't put my finger on. It bothered me that I couldn't figure him out.

I looked around, observing the party. There was a hand full of people in the covered patio in the backyard of the beautiful three-story home. A pool was back toward the woods, a Jacuzzi beside it, and a fireplace. I could only imagine the types of parties they had here.

I sat down next to Tisa at one of the round tables placed in their back yard. Clay sat across from me playing footsies, of course. I rolled my eyes at him but couldn't help but laugh right after. He was cute, charming, and a breath of fresh air. I wanted to breathe him again. I wanted to get lost in him.

The night consisted of an entrée prepared by a personal chef, a glass of wine, and open bar if desired. I was probably one of the youngest in attendance, but they welcomed me as if I was family. It made me feel like I mattered, even at a time when I didn't matter that much to the man I loved. It was temporary, but I took it all in for what it was. There were speeches made in honor of the individuals that made this film possible and a few surprise awards to people I didn't know but took a mental note of. Overall, I had fun. I smiled a lot more than I thought I would. I innocently flirted with older men and exchanged compliments with the women there. Everything was a success, and everyone was happy.

Throughout the night, I couldn't help but think of Clay. I barely knew him, but he was all I could think about. I just kept looking over at him while he interacted with everyone. He was naturally charming and a social butterfly, and I wanted a man that could make me feel comfortable in any situation. It made me warm inside. I sent a text for him to stop by my place tonight after the party, hoping I wouldn't later regret it. Once he saw the text he looked up at me and smiled and sent a reply saying he'd love to. He didn't ask about Dale even though the last he knew, I was in a relationship. He simply agreed, no questions asked, letting me take control and I loved it.

Tisa of course noticed that we were locking eyes and whispered in my ear, "He's a nice guy. Try him out, Noel. You may end up liking him."

I just nodded and looked away. I'm not exactly sure why she wanted me to get so close to him. She was always saying that business and pleasure weren't a good mix. But if she approved, I guess I would give him a shot. Granted, she didn't know that I already tried him out behind her back. She was older, wiser, and knew me well. I trusted her instinct. I'm not exactly sure where Dale and I were now, but it no longer concerned me. I let it go and made way for Clayton.

CHAPTER NINE

Clayton beat me to my house after the dinner party. I pulled up on the side of his Mustang and got out. He rushed out of his car and pulled the door open for me. I thanked him and led him into my home. I took my heels off at the door and watched him remove his dress shoes.

"Don't you live with someone?"

I was waiting for that. I led him around the house, avoiding his question.

"You sure do pose a lot of questions, Mr. Davis. Tell me why that is."

He looked down at his feet and looked back up at me.

"You're just a very mysterious woman. I'm trying to read you and I can't."

"Does that bother you?" I asked sarcastically. I wouldn't dare tell him I felt the same way about him. "Look around," I said as I watched his eyes glance around my condo, his eyes following my hand. "He lives here, he just isn't here right now."

He shook his head up and down and sucked his teeth.

"Well, is he coming back?"

I shrugged. "Maybe, but I'm betting that he won't. It's nothing to be concerned about. If he comes back it'll only be to get his clothes. I'm sure he won't bother us. Do you have any other questions?"

He shook his head no and grabbed my hand.

"You're tough, I like that." He then looked me in the eyes. I couldn't help but blush and show my teeth. "It's OK to get comfortable. I can tell that once the wall you have up falls, you'll be as sweet as pie." He put his hand on my heart. "You're soft. Not in a bad way, but fragile."

I looked away from him. Once again, my emotional side was being brought out of me. What the hell! I grew angry, then frustrated, then sensitive all over again. He saw it in my eyes and held me close. There we were, in the middle of the living room holding each other, not letting go, and I was on the verge of tears. I released myself from his embrace and locked the front door. Walking toward the stairs, I motioned for him to follow me up to the bedroom. On the bed there was a piece of a paper folded neatly. I picked it up and saw that it was from Dale and put it on the dresser. I'd read it tomorrow. He wasn't going to mess my night up. If it was that urgent, he would have contacted me on my cell phone.

"It's OK to be emotional every once in a while, Noel," Clayton said as he stood behind me over the bed, kissing my neck. "Soldiers cry too, you don't have to be so hard all the time."

I stood in silence as he turned me around and watched me cry. He let the tears fall and didn't ask any questions. Then he wiped my tears and kissed me softly on my lips.

"I'm here for you, this isn't an act. I don't secretly want to hurt you." He said softly in between deep breaths. I stopped to breathe. We were having a serious conversation, but the way he was looking at me made me hot. It was sexy and innocent.

"A guy told me that when I was in 9th grade when he was trying to get some pussy." I started to laugh, eyes still wet. "I'm sorry, I'm just not the type to just believe everything you say. You have to show me." I touched his nose as he looked up at me while pulling off my dress. He told me to be quiet and I listened.

"If all I wanted from you was sex, believe me, I would have lost interest that night at Hocking Hills."

I smiled sarcastically.

"Don't you want more?" He stopped what he was doing to laugh with me. We just sat there in that same position laughing for a minute straight. I enjoyed him. I enjoyed him a lot. It came to me as a surprise that after I just had my heart broken by Dale I could be sitting here about to make love to Clayton like it never happened. When I was with him, I forgot about the bad things. 24 hours ago, you would have never been able to tell me that I'd be here in the bedroom that I shared with whom I thought was the love of my life with another man. It's almost like I didn't even know myself anymore. I was changing for sure, but I'm not sure if it was for the better or for worse. Right now, I was just hoping that something great would come from this. With Clayton, not only was this messy, but it was putting my profession at risk. One wrong move and I could fuck up my position, lose a friend, and possibly an employee. This was a very delicate situation and instead of leaving it alone I decided to play with fire, and Lord knows I couldn't afford to get burned.

We made sweet love all night long and while I dreamt of us spending the weekend cuddled up, sexing, watching movies, baking cookies, and enjoying alone time, Dale showed up. I'm not sure if it was just me dreaming or if it was real. He was quiet as a mouse and didn't make a sound. I mean, he did still live here and have a key. It's not that I cared, I just didn't expect him so soon. Turning over, Clayton was sound asleep with his arm around my back. Something told me to open my eyes. I looked up into the hallway leading out of the bed room and saw Dale standing there in disbelief. I was startled, I won't lie. I didn't jump or get up, my body laid still. I didn't want to wake Clay and it turn into an altercation. I just stared at him. He was a distance away, but I saw the hurt in his eyes. I was glad he got to experience the same feeling I felt. After a while he just turned away and left. It was like he saw a ghost. Whether it was reality or just a dream, he was no longer there when I woke up. I looked over at Clayton's back as the sun shined in on it through the window. I was so love drunk it made no sense. I was embarrassed. I couldn't stop smiling.

Easing myself out of bed, I headed to the bathroom to shower and brush my teeth. I'd cook him breakfast, but I didn't know what he liked, so I decided to straighten up the house until he woke then propose taking him to breakfast, on me. It wasn't long before he came walking down the stairs smiling at me as if he saw me walking down the aisle on our wedding day. He was shirtless and man he looked good. His skin was so chocolate, and his teeth were so white. He was one of those guys that belonged on the cover of a magazine. I offered breakfast, but he politely declined. He had a prior engagement that he was committed to. I respected a man that kept his word, so I made no fuss. He kissed my forehead as he walked out the door and I got butterflies all over again. I slid to the floor smiling, high and happy.

CHAPTER TEN

There were 24 hours in a day, correct? It was now 2:00 PM, I suddenly decided that I wasn't going to be sitting in the house all sad, upset, and heartbroken. Hell no! I 23 years old and in my prime, I shouldn't be crying in my spare time. Fuck that. There was a sudden urge to get sexy and get a few drinks. It was game time and I wanted to see if I still had the juice. When I was 18, I could get anyone that I wanted. But over the years I settled down and damn near became a housewife to a mother fucker who couldn't even strap up when he cheated. These were my golden years and although I was feeling Clayton, he would *not* be my only option, especially after the mess that just happened with Dale.

I called up my good friend, Paisley, to go shopping with me. She was fine as hell, thick, and about her money. We haven't really hung out in a while. I mean we were both grown with busy schedules. I pretty much devoted my life to Dale and school, so we didn't really link up very often. That was all about to change. Paisley decided not to go to school but that had no weight on her career. She was 24 and a traveling freelance makeup artist. She made about $800 a week, built up her credit, and was on her way to becoming a homeowner. She was newly single, just got out of a relationship with a drug dealer. We would text every now and then to stay updated on each other's lives, so I knew a little bit of what was going on with her. Today would be good, sort of like therapy. I could get her caught up with my life and have a little fun. I picked her up in the Tahoe wearing some nice cheeky shorts, a crop top, some shades, and studded sandals.

"Bitchhhhhhhhhhhhhhhhhhhhhhhhh! When did you get this?!" she asked as she walked around the truck. "You look like me two years ago when Danny hit that lick!"

We both burst into laughter. Danny was her ex-boyfriend that was currently in the justice center facing charges. They were broken up before he got sentenced but remained roommates until he went away.

"I mean what can I say? I got a promotion."

She looked at me and tipped her sunglasses down. "Either they upped your pay tremendously or you started tricking on the side, which is it?"

I just laughed harder. She knew I wasn't getting paid that much working for Tisa, and even if I was, she also knew that I wasn't going to blow money on a truck I couldn't afford. There were more important things. She knew I was smart.

"Dale got it for me."

She took her glasses off and looked at me, her face glistening and clear. Part of being a makeup artist is having good natural skin too.

"But y'all broke up, right? Girl what's going on?" She looked so concerned and confused. I kept my eyes on the road and told her we'd discuss it over lunch because I was liable to crash the truck telling her while driving.

We decided to go to Friday's since they had some nice cheap drinks and the food was affordable. I was starving, but being smart, I only ordered artichoke dip as a starter. By the time I gave her the details of what was going on in my life, my appetite had come and gone. She ordered the Cajun chicken pasta and complained about how it used to taste better years ago. I thought that I would immediately dive into what happened recently, but I was so damn embarrassed. I had never been this embarrassed before, especially with her. She was damn near my best friend, the closest friend I had ever really had. Usually things of this matter would have been a piece of cake. I slowed down on my dip and focused on her before the waitress passed our table and took our drink order.

"Talk to me babe. So, what happened? You said you all weren't together any longer, then you pull up in a brand-new off-white Tahoe and tell me he bought it for you. I'm no longer following."

I took a deep breath, "Well… we are no longer together, that's for sure. *But…* he bought it for me a few weeks ago. We were fine then of course."

She just looked at me while sipping her water. The table was quiet while the waitress brought us our drinks. I got a top shelf long island and she ordered a Kahlúa and cream on ice. I pulled out my phone and found Dale's girlfriend and now child's mother's Instagram page and showed it to her.

"Who is she? His side piece?"

I told her to look through her pictures. It took a few seconds but when she saw the picture, she sat my phone down gently and slid it to the middle of the table. She stared into space and just said, "Oh."

I nodded slowly.

"And what makes the situation worse, is a few days before I found this out, I cheated on him with our new employee. I actually did get a promotion." I chuckled. "I felt so bad for doing it because all of these years I have never thought about looking at another man. Then I came home... wait, let me backtrack. He didn't even call me while I went on a mini vacation up the road with the other nigga. I came home and found some red lace panties and a condom, I'm assuming they didn't belong to his baby's mom. So, I left and got a room at the Courtyard in Blue Ash, met another nice guy, woke up in the morning and just so happened to call him, ya know, because I was beginning to get worried since he hadn't called me. I sent a text and got no reply. So, I looked on Instagram and here he likes *her* pictures. So, I clicked, and *boom*. I realized he had a whole different family. I was so worried about that Trinitee bitch, I didn't even see what was right in front of my face. *Oh!* And when I got home, he acted as though everything was alright."

She shook her head in disbelief. "He's a sorry ass excuse for a man." I agreed and continued with my story.

"He left after I revealed to him that I knew about it and came back the next night while my new guy was in the bed with me. He didn't say anything, just walked out of the room and left. At first, I thought I was dreaming, but he texted me and confirmed that he saw us and that he was so sorry, but what I did was low and cold. I was a whore and that I probably was cheating and thotting years ago. I reminded him that I found the rubber and the panties, so he should probably try again with that guilt trip shit."

I was out of breath. I was speaking so fast and I realized the volume of my voice had raised. She was quiet and still. She understood because she had been there before. She was my friend and whether she was quiet or responsive, she showed her respect and was supportive.

"I think you need a day off babe." She said as she grabbed my hand. "You need something wild and adventurous. You've been in the housewife role for quite some time. You need to have some fun. So, with that being said, there's a party later. It's a cat named Tommy. A friend of mine. I used to sneak and geek with him a while back but he always had his eyes on me and well you know, out of respect for her, he never approached me. Anyways, they no longer mess around, in fact, she up and moved to Cali on his ass and her and myself don't really associate so I consider him free game."

"Paisley! You can't do that!" I said while chuckling.

"Why the hell not!? None of these broads cared about me when it came to any of these niggas. He's free game! But see there's a twist."

I just looked at her with concern. Ever since Danny got locked up, Paisley had been mischievous about what she did and how she did it. I wasn't so sure that all her money came from her doing makeup.

"So, he wants to offer a nice amount to watch me and another young lady get intimate." I laughed so hard I almost spit out my drink. Then I realized that I was the young lady she was planning to get intimate with.

"Wait, me? You want to fuck me?"

She nodded her head yes. "It's not that bad Noel, and since I know you, it will be a bit easier. Maybe a little awkward at first but you'll get used to it. You don't have to go down on me or anything, I'll keep you satisfied."

I just sat there in awe. I've never touched another woman before. I'm not going to lie, I've thought about it and I get aroused when I see a nice looking woman, but I've never put those thoughts into action. Dale was not the type that wanted his girl dipping and dabbing with another woman.

"How much is he offering?"

She smiled a very grim smile and spoke softly. "Three bands just to watch. And since you're not doing any real work, I'll give you one."

I looked at her with big open eyes. "You aren't going to cheat me bitch! I need one point five! Just like you. 50/50, nothing more nothing less. I've never done anything like this before, so I need all my money."

She shook her head. "I get two you get one, that's final. You want 50/50 money, you do 50/50 work. Besides, you may meet a baller there that can take care of you, so consider this networking." She winked at me and smiled again.

"OK fine. Deal." I can't believe I just agreed to let someone like a best friend eat my pussy in front of a stranger. But I needed that money. Who knows what would happen between me and Dale based off recent events. If I could do this and pocket this money, then I'd put it in my savings as just in case money. Now usually I would have been a little more worrisome, but I trusted her. I knew she wouldn't do anything super dangerous, especially involving herself, but I did have one question to ask.

"So, that's all? He just wants to watch you eat me out and then we leave?"

She sipped her drink and assured me that I didn't have to do anything else. We shook on it and I began to mentally prepare myself for the wild shit I was going to do later. I was excited to do this because of my secret obsession with women. Yes, I know I'm smart and a young professional, but I'm human as well. I enjoy the woman's anatomy and physical being. Now as far as being emotionally attached to a woman, I don't think I'd be so willing. This was just what I needed to move forward, mentally and financially. The waitress brought us our checks and we paid for our meal. Paisley was smart which was part of the reason why we clicked in the first place. I turned to her as we left.

"So, is this what you do in your spare time to make extra money?"

She laughed. "It is. I've made a lot more disposable income based of little shit like this. I don't live above my means and I still work on my craft, so I'll never really be broke, even if I don't touch a makeup brush in a year. I'm going to teach you the game, so you can be up like me, but for now, let's go shopping and find something for tonight. I nodded and followed her to the car. Checking my phone, I saw a text message from Clayton who was just checking up on me. I decided to not respond and to call him later. I had been seeing him more than casually and I wanted to make him continue to sweat me like he was doing initially. If a man sees you too often, he gets bored, and that's the last thing I wanted. So, I thought with all the Ls I've taken with him, and every man that I deal with for that matter, I can do some damage control and put the ball back in my court. It will all work out in the end.

CHAPTER ELEVEN

It had been months since I stepped foot in Paisley's apartment. I almost forgot what it looked like. She upgraded and did some redecorating. Everything was so girly and cute; the way a young single woman's place should look. Her favorite color was red, so you could probably guess that everything was on one accord. She accented her home with gold, so it gave me royal vibes. I loved it! She had a vanity in her guest room where she did makeup that was to die for. Yes, I had more space, yes, I had two floors, yes, my condo was more expensive, but her apartment was laid from her interior decorating and she had more disposable income. Being here made me realize that you don't have to live beyond your means to live comfortably. Hell, my condo didn't have the slightest bit of interior decorating, it was bland. It looked as if we just moved in. It wasn't home. Paisley's apartment felt like home. It was warm and had a hint of luxury. I wanted that in my life. Warmth, intimacy, and a sense of home. You don't have to prove anything to anyone, in fact, you should act like you're broke and save up. My friend has so much money but lives a regular lifestyle, no one would ever know. That's what I admired about her. She wasn't pressed to prove that she had money and she didn't care if people knew. In fact, she didn't want anyone to know. And most of all, she wasn't going to settle for modern day luxuries.

—

And here I was, taking a nigga's shit for years all because he gave me everything I asked for. Behind all the materialistic possessions, I was miserable. I had nice things, I wanted for nothing, and I was being taken care of, but I was missing out on more important things. I had no mental or emotional peace from worrying and keeping up with who he was dilly dallying around with. My house was not a home. The only memories that I have there are being alone. Dale was never there and when he was, it was brief. It got to the point where I didn't even ask where he had been or who he was with. I knew those nights he was out late weren't because of overtime. I found out recently that they were from him having a child on the way. He had to comfort the mother of his child during her pregnancy. I became the other woman years ago when I first asked him about Trinitee. Nothing changed after posing the question. I didn't leave him or anything. And it only progressed from there. Now he's moved on to bigger and better things, like starting a family behind my back. Maybe I should have held off on taking that Plan B. But then again, that would make me just like her and in competition for a man that would never change. And if he did change, it would be no time soon and not for the sake of me. I say that to say this; trust your intuition. I may have been off as far as who he was spending his time with, but I knew he wasn't at work. For all I know, he could have been with both her and Trinitee. The possibilities were limitless, but I'd rather not entertain them.

All his bullshit put me in the mood to make some money and boss up. I was still mentally and emotionally drained. Shit, I was broken and confused but I learned at an early age that looking for closure didn't always help, so I went with the flow and let things happen the way they did. I wanted to figure out the next steps with myself and Dale, but I was living comfortably so there was no rush. I wanted to figure Clay out, but obviously that too needed time. And yes, I wanted to flourish in my career but of course Rome wasn't built in a day. Things took time and I was OK with that. For now, I was going do what I had to do and make it work on my end.

—

"Mmmm, let's do a natural look on you! A dramatic eye and nude lip will pop for you!" Paisley was literally the G.O.A.T of makeup. Whatever she wanted to do, I was certainly here for. We ended up buying silk black dresses that had a dropped chest area. They were slimming and complemented our figure. She was of fairer skin and I was brown, a shade just under chocolate. She was literally the opposite of me. She had a larger bottom and I had bigger breasts. Both of us had flat stomachs and dominant features. My legs were one of my great qualities, as well as my cheekbones. My forehead was a bit smaller than average, but my lips were full and flawless. My nose, unlike hers, was something I'd always been insecure about, it was longer and pointy whereas hers was small like a button. She did in fact have a big forehead like most light skin women did and a fat face, but we both had some straight pearly whites. Her being my best friend and makeup artist, I knew she would know how to complement my features. My eyes were my prized possession and I trusted her to bring them out without being overly dramatic.

She put the mirror up to my face and showed me the finished product. Truthfully, I damn near cried. I loved it! She accented my eyes with green eyeliner, gave me a nude lip gloss, and gold eyelids. I looked like I was about to tie the knot. I thanked her and went to get dressed.

"Our flight leaves at 9:00 so I'm giving you 30 minutes," she said as she touched up her makeup. I stepped backward from the bathroom with half of my dress up.

"Our flight?!" Flight to where?"

She laughed at me and gave me a look that made it seem like I forgot about something.

"You didn't think this was happening in Cincinnati, did you? We're going to New York baby. Tommy moved to New York." She continued to do her makeup.

I was motionless, silent, and still. "Paisley, I have to work tomorrow, I didn't know that we were going out of town." She continued to do her makeup and apply lipstick. When she was finished, she patted her lips together and finally spoke.

"Hey, hey calm down. He bought us plane tickets there and back, you'll be back in the morning at 8:00. You said you didn't work until noon. I pay attention. For now, let's just focus on having fun. This is a rooftop social, I'm sure there will be very important people here. But then again, you deal with important people daily, so you'd fit right in. We're just going to lounge around for a few and once it's over we're going to go up to his loft and that's where it's all going down."

I just looked at her blank faced.

"So, you trust this man enough to have him fly us to New York and get kinky for him in his loft?"

She shook her head and told me she had slept with him on a few occasions. She used him as a get away from time to time. I let my guard down and decided to go. I didn't trust him, but I trusted her, so I agreed to tag along. Pulling my dress up, I made my way into the bathroom, admiring my beauty. I hadn't *felt* this pretty in a long time. It's more than looking the part, you have to truly feel it. I was flawless. And I deserved more than a good time, I was getting ready to fly to New York for the first time and attend an upscale social. Who knows who I'd meet, who knows what would happen. I was excited. But then I thought about how we were going to be whores later tonight. It didn't bother me when I thought about it more, because I wasn't fucking anyone. I mean, I was letting her eat my box for a band, but I didn't have to do anything. I took a deep breath and got my mental together. This will be fun, I thought to myself. I'll enjoy myself. Paisley yelled that she was ready, and I followed her down the steps into the Uber that took us to the airport. This was the beginning of something new.

CHAPTER TWELVE

Paisley snatched the headphones out of my ears. "Noel you're going to get left on the plane if you don't get up."

I opened my eyes to see that majority of the other passengers had gathered their carry-on bags and were headed off of the plane.

"Shit!" I grabbed my carry-on and stood behind Paisley. I didn't realize how tired I really was until I was able to relax for more than five minutes. There was no memory of the plane ride, just boarding and waking up. We were here, LaGuardia airport. I was ecstatic but didn't want to seem lame. I take it that in the time that we were distant, Paisley did this often. Especially since her and Danny were no longer together.

"So what part of New York does he live in?" I asked as we entered the terminal.

"Manhattan! But we have to stop in Queens, so I can introduce you to my girl Perez. You'll love her!" Paisley was very monotone, but when she was excited, she was also very extra. It was weird. She painted pictures with her words poetically and was always very descriptive when she talked. She was one of those people that said everything through her facial expressions. Even if she was trying to be discrete, it never worked in her favor because everything was expressed in her face before a single word was spoken.

"How long have you known her?" I asked, just making conversation. I really didn't care how long she knew the broad, I was starving and was ready to get this night over with and go home with my cash. I wasn't moody at all, just eager and anxious. The faster we could do this, the faster I could get back to work and see Clayton, and the faster I could relax in my own bed.

We caught a cab from the airport to Queens, so we could see Paisley's home girl Perez. She was more than attractive. She wore her hair in a top bun while her baby hair lay on the sides of her face and behind her ears. Perez was a New York native so the style came naturally. She was gorgeous! Slim and short with the right amount of everything. Her accent was heavy, but she had a bit of southern twang to her as well. She welcomed us inside her home and gave me a big hug.

"Hey pretty girl! Any friend of Paisley is a friend of mine. So nice to meet you darling! I've heard so many good things." I hadn't really heard anything about her but I'm sure if I were to say that, the mood of the room would be awkward, so I lied.

"I've heard so many things about you as well! It's nice to finally meet you!"

Paisley gave me the side eye once I responded. She knew I was lying through my teeth. Before the conversation went left, she took the attention away from me with some small talk amongst her and her friend.

"So, Perez, what's new with you and Peter?"

Perez just rolled her eyes and walked toward the kitchen.

"I'm sorry who?"

We all giggled. Even though I had the slightest idea of who this Peter person was, I still thought it was funny. Obviously, she knew him, but he had to really fuck up for her to her to deny his existence. We've all been there. I'm sure if someone asked if I knew Dale, I'd do the same thing. I don't even want to think about him. I wish I had never met him at this point.

"You ladies look so gorgeous by the way. Paisley you are just getting better by day. You think you'd have time to get me together?" Paisley was drinking water and had to swallow before responding.

"Yes I could! You should come with us! It'll be fun!" Perez just side eyed her and shook her head.

"Absolutely not my darling," she said in an angelic voice.

I wondered why she made it so clear that she didn't want to go to the party. Paisley just said OK, but in the back of my mind, my suspicion wouldn't go away.

"Why don't you want to go?"

She looked at me and then smiled. "Not my type of party, and honestly… I'm not fond of Tommy. We grew up together. He did a complete 360."

My face pretty much said everything that I was thinking. I was confused because Paisley said Tommy was from Cincinnati.

"I thought you said he was from Cincy?"

Paisley shook her head. "No, I said that he was living in Cincinnati, but he moved back here. Pay attention kid, you need your listening skills if you're going to try to wow someone tonight and pick their pockets. You might find a nice away from home sugar daddy and you're messing up small details. Come on Noel, get it together and fast. These guys up here are slick. Don't let anyone talk you out your panties without running you a check first."

I sat silently reflecting on this whole situation as they both laughed and chopped it up while Paisley did her makeup. Maybe I wasn't listening, but I could have sworn she said that he was from Ohio.

—

We left Perez's apartment shortly after Paisley finished touching up her makeup. This woman I called my friend really had me questioning her. I was stuck on the fact that I was so sure that she told me that this Tommy guy was from our city. I didn't press it, but it did in fact bother me. The fact that Perez was so un-eager to come along made me question things as well. I just kept wondering what the hell was I about to get myself into. I have never tricked or did anything sexual in front of a man for money. I was nervous, but I wanted the money and to have more control over my future. I had to find stability again – financially, mentally, and emotionally.

I swallowed my butterflies during the Uber ride to Manhattan. I know that Paisley felt the tension between us, but she said nothing. We rode in complete silence. This also bothered me, but I too remained quiet and observant. Thoughts of my scrambled love life fled my mind. I wanted so desperately to give in to Clayton, I was vulnerable. But I also wanted to patch things up with Dale. The bartender from the hotel also still lingered on my mind. Then at the same time, I wanted to learn to be independent again. I was lost, and somehow, I had to get myself out of this mess and fast. All these emotions and internal battles were really draining me mentally. I tried to brush these feelings off and show no weakness but the more I acted as though nothing was wrong, the more my mind and spirit grew empty. I don't need a temporary high, I need a permanent solution. As of now my longing for love and marriage was deteriorating. Only lust I had was for independence, freedom, stability, and the self-love.

This situation brought a lot out about me that I didn't know. I take that back, I knew, but I didn't shed light on these things. I kept them in the closet and locked the door. Over the years I became everything I said I'd never be. Slowly but surely, subconsciously, I gave up 99 percent of my life for a man and the "lifestyle" that was perceived by others as more than fortunate. On the outside looking in, I was well taken care of. And I was to a certain degree, but what matters most to me is the mind. Who gives a fuck what clothes you have and where you live if your state of mind is broken and drained. I'm not happy and to be honest I don't recall a time where I have been. Maybe I'll call my mother tomorrow. If I wanted to gain control of my life, it had to start somewhere. So, starting by mending our relationship would be the first on my list. Small steps that all contribute to the ultimate goal.

"Hey pay attention man! What the fuck? You almost killed us!" Paisley screamed, shaking me out of my thoughts. The Uber driver almost tipped the car over while trying to get off the expressway after almost missing our exit. His apologies were endless, sincere, and repetitive. He was tired, you could see it in his eyes. I wasn't angry, I was compassionate. Maybe he had a hard life and needed the extra money. That could be why he was falling asleep at the wheel. The recent events in my life made me soft. Paisley though, she was livid, cursing, and shouting.

"Chill," I told her, slightly raising my voice. She looked at me like I was bat out of hell crazy.

"What the fuck do you mean chill? We almost died. What the hell is wrong with you? He needs to chill obviously cau…" I stopped her.

"Here's $100, let this be your last ride for tonight, I know you could probably make more driving, but you need to get some rest, sir." I held out the money for him in my right hand.

"Bitch are you serious right now?! This motherfucker just almost killed us, and you are rewarding him? I can't believe this shit yo!" She shook her head and laughed sarcastically, mumbling under her breath. The Uber driver, Samuel, thanked me and began crying. He started to explain that he was trying to make extra money so that he and his son could eat which is why he fell asleep at the wheel and almost missed the exit. He worked three jobs to make ends meet in a studio apartment and had no money for food. I stopped him and told him that he didn't have to explain his situation to me and apologized for Paisley's outburst. We pulled up to our destination and got out. I looked at him one last time before he pulled off, he mouthed "thank you" and I smiled.

CHAPTER THIRTEEN

Checking my phone, I saw three text messages from Clayton
and a long single message from Dale. I was very tempted to
block him, but we still shared a home, and until we parted
ways I had to keep it saved. Opening the message, I saw that it
was a good paragraph or two and decided to read it once I was
settled in tonight. I didn't need any negative energy right now
and I wasn't going to let him cast an angry cloud upon me. I
opened Clayton's thread and saw a bunch of heart and kissing
emojis. The message following said, "I know you're probably
busy, but I'd like to take you out." Then the last one said,

"Send me your schedule and your measurements please. I want to plan a special day for us."

I thought on these messages. It almost seemed as if this was too easy. Now usually I wouldn't think this hard into a situation like this, but I liked Clayton. But what bothered me was that he was too charming to be this winded by me this fast and this easily. We slept together twice and it's like this nigga was seriously head over heels. I didn't understand it. Yes, I have a nice personality, I'm smart, and I'm attractive, but he was too dammit. I was literally starting to question everything. Nothing made sense right now. This man was fine as hell and he could get any woman that he wanted. Someone more established, a cougar that was willing to take care of him. But he wanted *me.* I wish someone would just make this all make sense. I was starting to think that something was wrong with him. Everyone starts out cool. Was he a dog? Did he have an STD? Was he manipulative? I made a mental note to go to the OBGYN when I got back home. I can't afford any slip ups and yet I was being so careless.

And then there was Tisa. For some odd crazy reason, she took special interest in him and I. This is Tisa we are talking about. I mean seriously, she didn't give a shit about my love life any other time, but for some reason, she was breathing over my shoulder every chance she got and encouraging me to give Clayton a chance. I was thinking too hard about all of this, so I just broke my thought process and simply responded, "Yes, I've been busy. I have my own money, tell me what the attire is, and I'll find something. Thank you for the offer though. I'll send my schedule over in the morning. Goodnight my love." Whatever was going on, I'm sure I'll figure it out sooner or later, but until then I'd let him get a little closer. I enjoyed his company and was hoping that being around him could help me get over Dale once and for all. I just wasn't sure if I wanted to create a new love cycle with him either.

—

"Hey there!" Paisley greeted a taller darker skinned man with a hug. We had just walked in the party and past the security when his white teeth damn near slapped me in the face. He was fine as hell, muscular, sexy, and clean. He had on a wine-colored button down and black slacks. Simple and attractive, very balanced, and just how I liked my men. I was seriously starting to think I was developing into a whore like Dale said. Every attractive man I saw, I day dreamed of sleeping with them and my flower became dripping wet between my thighs almost instantly. It was like her heartbeat was as fast as mine as I looked him up and down not trying to be too obvious that I was interested. Paisley looked at me and back to him and suddenly I caught drift of what she was doing.

"Hey, I'm Noel nice to meet you," I said softly breaking the silence. He leaned in for a hug, but I declined it and put my hand out, welcoming a more cordial handshake. He was already too comfortable, and I wasn't going to start this off that way. He was too attractive and charming, I had to let him know that I wasn't that easy. He laughed politely and smiled fixing his stance and extending his hand.

"Justin. It's definitely my pleasure." He took my hand and placed a single kiss on top of it and locked eyes as he let it go. Paisley smiled, even though she was well aware that I was questioning even being here with her right now and she was still thrown off by the Uber driver situation. She wasn't going to say anything about it though, she wasn't very confrontational. There wasn't much to say. Nothing she did or said would change the uneasiness I felt about this. But I didn't flee, so that implied that I would take the risk and find out if this feeling of sketchiness amounted to anything, or if it was just me being nervous and overthinking. As far as the Uber driver, I did what I felt was right. The man obviously was tired and shouldn't have been driving, so his actions were forgiven. I rather give him some extra money to take a damn nap than later hearing about him pushing himself too hard and killing himself at the wheel or worse, the individuals he was driving around. I wouldn't be able to live with myself knowing that I could have done something to help.

Meanwhile, Justin kept smiling at me and instead of it creeping me out like it would any other time, it kind of turned me on. I smiled and kept it moving, following Paisley away from him, but keeping my eye on him the further I got away.

"Nice call. There are plenty more men here to choose from. You didn't jump on the first man you saw, that was a good move." I just listened to Paisley talk. "Mingle as much as possible. Everyone here tonight is pretty much a baller, so you don't have to worry about any bullshit."

I just nodded as we walked through a maze of at least100 people to get to the bar. She was talking to me like we were on some super undercover mission trying to stay off radar. Almost like I had never been around any ballers in my life. Naturally, I took offense and became irritated, but I kept quiet about it. But I knew that as soon as we got home, we needed to talk, and I would explain why the way she acted tonight bothered me.

The bartenders were all very curvy and pretty in the face. They all had on fitted, elegant dresses and heels, and full faces of makeup that complemented their attire. I took a drink menu off the bar and looked over it. There were no regular club drinks on this menu, just restaurant type drinks and champagne. I ordered a southern mule which was one of my favorites. Back in the city, the only place that I knew of that had them was Longhorn Steakhouse, so I was a bit excited. I tried to give the bartender my card to purchase my drink, but she told me that a young man by the name of Justin already had an open tab on whatever I liked. A little shocked, I looked around trying to find him. Not because he put an open tab on my drinks, but because he did that in little to no time. Gazing around through the thick crowd of people, I spotted Justin in a corner looking at me. I smiled and sipped my mule, lifting it in the air as if I was saying cheers, waiting for him to approach me. To my surprise he didn't. I whispered to Paisley that I would be right back and began to walk in his direction. Normally I wouldn't have taken the drink, I'd be too afraid that someone had slipped something in it. But I watched the bartender from start to finish, and even if there was a quick way to slip something in it, Paisley saw everything, and she would know who did what and where. I had my doubts about tonight, but as far as my safety goes, I know she wouldn't let that be compromised. The closer I got to Justin the more nervous I became. He was mysterious and that excited me. I just could not understand why he was so interested in *me* out of all the beautiful, established women here tonight.

"Did you sprint to the bar and tell them to place anything I wanted on your open tab? Because when I walked away you went the other direction," I said sarcastically walking up on him. He laughed and couldn't help but smile when he talked.

"Well, I'm pretty well plugged in. All I have to do is send a text. Where are you from? This is my first time seeing you around here."

I kept a straight face and told him I was from Cincinnati. He went on to tell me how he'd never been there but heard a lot about it.

"Excuse me, but why the special interest?" I rudely interrupted him. He laughed again. He nodded his head slowly and stuck his lips out to the side.

"You're straight forward, eh?" He chuckled once more but I kept a straight face. Once he realized that I wasn't amused, he got serious.

"I've been watching you since you got out of your Uber and walked into this party. The way you carry yourself caught my interest and the vibe I got upon meeting you told me that I should try to get to know you."

At this point I just laughed, hysterically. He looked at me with confusion but stood quietly waiting patiently for me to finish. I cleared my throat and apologized if I offended him.

"You can get to know me." I stated. He just looked at me blank faced for a while. It made me uncomfortable. I started to feel embarrassed. He finally spoke.

"How long are you in town?"

I hesitated when I spoke. Shit he made me nervous.

"I leave in the morning. I have to get back to work tomorrow evening." He asked what type of work I did. I told him I was a screen-writer, but I was interning for Tisa Daniels. I didn't have to tell him who she was. He nodded and smiled immediately.

"Nice. I'm sure you'll end up great working with her."

Tisa was a popular up and comer. A lot of people knew her work but didn't know who she was by appearance. She stayed low key for the most part and she was just starting to get recognition.

"I'm assuming you have experience in film? You act like you know her personally." He looked at me and smiled.

"I know a lot of people, but no, no film experience. I own properties and flip houses. She used to date my uncle. Ask her about Robert Jackson and tell her you met his nephew once you get back. Now that you say that, I can see that you've been under her supervision. That's a good thing! She is an extraordinary woman like yourself." He handed me his business card. "Give me a call when you land, I won't keep you. I know you have to go back to Paisley. Just enjoy yourself tonight and don't forget to call. I hope to see you soon." He kissed my hand again and half bowed to me. His lips were so warm and soft. I told him I would call him as he requested, and we parted ways.

On the way back to Paisley, I began to think and wondered how he even knew her. We were at this party to trick. I know it sounds bad but shit, that's pretty much what it was. Did she meet him here? I guess she had to, being that he'd never been to Cincinnati. They just seemed very well acquainted and that made me question what terms they met on. Shoot, he probably spent some money with her too. This wasn't the Paisley that I knew. She just seemed really money hungry, like a leach or a sack chaser. You can about your money without being thirsty. She was being a little too thirsty for my comfort.

—

There were people everywhere. All types of people. Black, white, Asian, Middle Eastern, all dressed up and glowing. I had never been to an event like this. It was something I'm glad I attended. People here admired me, I saw it in the way people looked at me. I know I'm attractive, but these men and even some women looked almost astonished by me. I wasn't as formal as everyone else, so I didn't quite understand why I was being scouted out. Nothing to ponder too hard on though. I caught up to Paisley talking to a larger brown skinned man with moles all over his face.

"Noel, this is Tommy. He's the one responsible for us being here." I smiled at him and took his hand for a shake. I noticed he had moles all over his skin, not just his face. It was a unique feature.

"It's nice to finally meet you. Thank you for your hospitality. This is a very nice event!" He thanked me for honoring him with my presence. He showed us around the rooftop venue and led us to a secluded area in the back. He gave us two paper contracts. I looked up at Paisley, and then back at him.

"What the hell is this?" I began to read over it. "A non-disclosure? What the fuck do I need to sign this for? She's just eating some pussy right?"

Paisley's eyes got big and she told me to be quiet. Tommy smiled a very creepy smile and assured me that that was still the plan but because of who he is and what he does, there couldn't be any accidents or public notification of this going on.

"I can assure you the last thing on my mind is telling anyone I took part in formal prostitution." I sat the paper down and returned his pen. "I'm not signing anything. You can either trust me like I'm trusting you to give me my money and not try anything that I don't agree to or that wasn't originally discussed, or you can dismiss me from your event and I'll purchase my own ticket back to Cincinnati."

Tommy just looked at Paisley without saying a word. I'm assuming he wanted her to calm me down. But she knew that once my mind was set to something there no reason in trying. I looked down at her in disgust as I got up from the couch and adjusted my dress.

"Now if you'll excuse me, thank you for the opportunity but no thanks." I walked past him to leave the party. I was *pissed*. Not because I was missing out on money, but because my friend was going to sign a non-disclosure just to give a bitch some head. I know close to nothing about this type of business but from the few stories that I've heard, they drug you and do whatever they want with you. Fuck that! I'm not selling my soul for a thousand dollars. Hell, I could very well be overreacting, but I wasn't taking any chances because if something like that did happen, even if he assured it wouldn't I wouldn't be sober enough to know to stop it and neither would she. No thank you. And signing a legal binding document for confidentiality wasn't smart when in the terms there was nothing about using no drugs. Nope, I wasn't going to do it. I stormed out of the party and ran straight into Justin.

"Shit, I'm sorry I didn't even see you!" I said before even realizing that it was him. "I guess everything happens for a reason because I was just about to call you."

He smiled showing his perfect white teeth.

"Is that right? You are ditching your friend?"

I shook my head. "No, she decided to stay but I'm tired. I was going to go to a hotel until the morning. I was wondering if you could recommend one for me. This is my first time here." He grabbed my hand and we began walking.

"You can stay the night at my place tonight, I'm only around the corner."

I stopped him dead in his tracks. "Thanks for your offer, but I'm not interested. I don't know you and I don't feel comfortable staying in your apartment overnight." He looked offended.

"Who said I had an apartment? I have a house. But I understand, I shouldn't have approached you like that and for that I apologize and will take care of the hotel for you." His eyes were expressive like mine. I stood there for a moment before responding.

"I don't need you to do that, I just want a recommendation. Thank you but I will certainly be OK." He pulled me close to him. He was taller than me, so naturally I had to look up as he was speaking. Hoping his breath didn't smell, I gave him my full attention.

"I'll take you to your hotel. Please, it's the least can do for offending you."

Yes! It didn't smell like anything, so I let my guard down a little. I know, I know, weird. But if he would have opened up his mouth that close to my nose and his breath smelled, I would have taken that as bold disrespect and my answer would have been a definite no.

"OK, fine. Lead the way." I said as he wrapped his arm around me and led me to the corner where his limo driver opened the door for us to step inside.

CHAPTER FOURTEEN

I had never been to New York. I didn't have any friends that lived there and hadn't really heard too much about it other than the typical saying, "The city that never sleeps." But actually, being here was breathtaking. I've done my fair share of traveling but I had never been somewhere so busy and alive. I'm from a small town where everyone knows everyone, so in a setting like this, I truly fell in love. My time was occupied with looking out the window and sightseeing from the car. Justin just sat beside me glancing at the partition occasionally.

He was quiet. I read him as respectful, handsome, and reserved. He made me nervous though. Not the type of nervous that instilled fear, but the type of nervous that gave me butterflies. There was a strong possibility that I would grow to like and care for him. That made me question inviting him to stay the night with me. If I did, I'd have to immediately cut all ties with him. The guys that are usually no good always start off charming and respectful.

"Where are we going?" I asked him, realizing that he didn't even ask what hotel I was thinking of staying at. He gave me the sexiest smirk.

"Patience. I thought you'd enjoy a stay at my favorite hotel," he said softly while gently rubbing the top of my hand. It tickled so I involuntarily moved my hand over to my thigh. "Am I making you uncomfortable?" he asked.

"No, I'm just ticklish." He laughed which forced me to smile. I didn't have the best sense of humor, which is why a lot of people initially painted an evil picture of me. But upon getting acquainted you'll realize I'm actually goofy and entertaining. Out of the corner of my eye, I saw him admiring my beauty. He would smile, as if I made him happy. I turned my head away from the window and in his direction to see if he'd turn away. He didn't, he just kept admiring.

"If I didn't know any better, I'd think you were sweet on me." I winked at him.

"Does that surprise you?" A question being answered with a question was usually sarcasm. Remaining quiet, I sat and thought. First off, I'm sure he had very expensive taste, so maybe his recommended hotel wasn't such a great idea. But of course, I knew that upon asking him. I could have found an inexpensive hotel and kept it pushing and called him tomorrow like he asked. Subconsciously, I wanted to be around him tonight. I had money but due to the circumstances that I was in, I wasn't prepared to go off the deep end spending too much out here. I wasn't supposed to be spending anything at all. The entire reason that I was here was to make money. That didn't go as planned, so I basically just came to spend more money. I'm sure that he planned to pay for this hotel room even though I told him I could handle it. I'm prepared to say no, because well, then he's going to want something in return and I'm not sure giving him some ass right after meeting him is going to give him a good impression. I wanted him to remember me, not just when he gets bored and horny. I wanted him to long to be around me, to genuinely want my presence.

"It's just your energy." He interrupted my thoughts. "Your energy makes me want to get to know you, I mean really get to know *you*. I gravitate toward people like you, and looking past your tough exterior, I can tell that you're pure gold." I smiled at him.

"Likewise." I didn't want to stroke his ego and I'm sure there were women everywhere throwing themselves at him. He had money too, so that probably tripled his numbers and his chances.

We pulled up at the Mandarin Oriental New York. I had never even heard of this place, but it was beautiful. I tried to get out and open the door, so I could book my room, but he held me back.

"I'll take care of it." This is what I didn't want to happen, although I knew it was coming and really appreciated it. I know by the looks of this place that it was not in my budget, but I didn't want to embarrass myself and have to make an excuse last minute and find a different hotel.

"You know I would have been fine staying at a Marriott. I didn't need anything fancy. I'll only be here for one night." He told me to hush and got out of the car to make a call. I just heard him say, "Yes the central park skyline suite." He went in the lobby and came back out with a keycard and told me to follow him.

Our room was on the 45th floor. I felt like a damn child at a candy factory. In the back of my mind, I couldn't help but think about him wanting something in return. I wanted to give it to him, but I didn't want to be just another body in his collection. He was charming, and I could see a future with him. I didn't want it to end after one night. I didn't know what to do, but I had to think fast. I really wanted to just say fuck it and bring it to his attention that I wasn't interested in sleeping with him. I didn't want to seem weak in admitting that I was afraid that after I gave it to him he would lose interest and fall back. He may be offended, after all he was very respectful. I've slept in the same bed as a man before who didn't try anything with me. I didn't want to go diving over the deep end.

I walked behind him slowly. My feet began to ache from walking. I hated heels without platforms because they made my feet hurt. He opened the door to what looked like a modern-day apartment. There was a couch to the left and a door to the right where the bedroom was. There was office space and a microwave above a sink and a kitchen without a stove top or oven. A small refrigerator and freezer sat on the counter. I didn't have any big bags, only a purse that I used as my carry on because I knew this would be a one-night thing and by time I got up to get dressed I'd be boarding the plane to go back to Ohio. He admired the view and I walked toward the bedroom. I sat on the bed and realized how comfortable it was. I took my heels off and moved my toes around. I let out a deep breath and got up to see what the bathroom looked like. Now, I was clearly amazed because I had never been in a hotel *this* nice before. I was stunned at the marble floors, the rainforest shower, and separate bath tub. There was even a powder room. I felt like a broke bitch even though back in Cincinnati I was looked at to be a bit of uppity. I had pretty much everything I wanted. Dale took care of me. But being here had me thinking twice about sticking around for him. It wasn't worth it. Clearly

Justin had money. I already knew that, but this was icing on the cake. This room didn't look cheap at all. I couldn't help but wonder how often he came here for leisure. I couldn't help but think I was selling myself short for being loyal to a cheater. I'd rather be a dumb bitch for Justin, at least he could invest and sponsor a business for me so that eventually I'd make my own bread and wouldn't be so dependent on him. Actually no, I don't want to be a loyal dumb ass to any man. I was worth more than the hush money he's given me, even if he was a billionaire. The emotional stress and hurt weighed out the dollar sign. I can't pretend that I truly love a man just because he can give me money. Naturally it's going to hurt knowing he is unfaithful, and he can just give me a gift, or a wad of cash and I'd overlook it.

"What do I owe you for this room?" I was just being polite, I had no intention of paying him anything for this. Maybe I shouldn't have asked and just took it for what it was without faking my concern because he looked very offended.

"Excuse me?"

I had to clean up what could have ended very badly.

"I mean this room obviously isn't cheap. We just met. You didn't have to go all out like this. Honestly, I would have been fine at a Marriott or something. I have to pay you back." He walked in the bathroom and stood behind me in the mirror. I regretted saying I had to pay him back almost instantly. To my surprise, he just pulled my hair behind my ears and looked me in the eyes in the mirror.

"I'm not concerned with expenses my love. You owe me nothing. I just wanted to take some time with you to get to know you a little better before you head back to Ohio. I'm not sure if I'll ever see you again, so I had to take advantage of the opportunity."

I turned to him and gave him a hug. From the look on his face and the way his body stood still, I could tell he was surprised. I kissed him on the lips, softly and quickly. I didn't even realize what I had just done until I stood back and began to blush. As chocolate as he was, I could see he was blushing too. I just laughed at that point. I was kind of embarrassed, but I liked it.

"I've been having a bad few weeks and I just really appreciate what you're doing for me. Consider that a thank you." Before he could respond, I turned to see plush terry bathrobes. "*Wow*! This hotel is so dope. I'm sorry if I sound like a broke hoe, I've just never been to a hotel as nice as this!" He just chuckled.

"It's all good. Believe me, my first time here I fell in love. Are you hungry?"

I stopped what I was doing to think. Shit, I was hungry. But he paid for everything else, so I didn't want him to keep coming out of pocket.

"I am hungry actually. What were you thinking about eating? It's on me." I turned back toward the robes, taking one off of the hanger to examine it.

"Come on girl, you don't think I'm going to let you buy me food, do you? That would be rude of me."

I interrupted him. "What would be rude of me is letting you spend all of this money when I have my own. It's OK, I'll handle it. Just tell me what you'd like I'll give you cash to go get it or I can call in an order." I began to undress not even thinking. I'm very comfortable with my body and I will strip almost anywhere, in front of almost anyone. You could tell he was trying to pay attention to what I was saying while I undressed but couldn't respond because of the distraction. I stopped, realizing what I was doing.

"Oops, I'm sorry. I'm just really comfortable with myself," I said grabbing the robe covering my almost nude body. I wore black lace panties and a lace bralette to match. My boobs were big but still perky. I loved the way they sat up in bralettes.

"We can dine in our room. I'm a pizza man. There's a pizza parlor around the corner that I like. I can run and get us some." I agreed and told him I'd get in the shower while he was away and handed him a $50 bill. I wasn't sure how much pizza was here, but it was New York so I had to be prepared. I also let him know that I was sending my location to my friend just in case he had any surprises. He assured me it wasn't that type of party but for my security I sent Paisley and Dale my location and followed up with an apology for not responding to his message earlier. I told him I was out of town with Paisley and just wanted to be safe and share my location with him. He responded instantly and told me to be safe and that we'd talk when I got home. Paisley responded and told me to be safe. She apologized and that we'd talk later. Justin left to grab the pizza and I stripped completely naked and stepped into the shower. The warm water made me feel refreshed. This felt like a new beginning and I was in love with the thought.

CHAPTER FIFTEEN

Justin was a temporary high. I wanted to get lost in him. I was so uptight about having sex with him earlier, I was taken aback when my thoughts wandered in another direction. As the water from the shower beat down on my body, I felt free. If we had sex, we had sex. That's how I felt at this very moment. I can't hide that he turned me on. I couldn't hide that from myself if I wanted to. I'm sure it was very clear to him that I wanted him sexually, even while acting like I didn't. I wasn't sure if I should just dive into it when he got back or if I should just try to avoid it. I was hot. I didn't even really understand it.

A few years ago, I would have never been in these types of situations. My life consisted of two things: Dale and my career. There was no time for me, and in turn, once I became mentally detached, I began to run wild. I'm lost though. I didn't take the time out to figure myself out, or what I liked, and what made me happy. I'm on the right path as far as my career is concerned, but I don't experience life the way I should. I was a direct reflection of my mother. I gave myself to a man and sacrificed my happiness to chase him around and now that it's over, I'm wishing that I could go back in time and change that. I keep surprising myself. Never in a million years would I have even thought about sleeping with another man. It just seems like the more time I spend away from Dale, the more aroused I get. Every attractive man I see that shows me interest, I imagine myself in bed with him. I want to know what he's like behind closed doors, if his sex is as good as he looks, and sometimes what a future would look like with him. It's like I'm in some sexual fantasy world. I can't even say I'm just fantasizing about these men sexually, it's more than that. I'm fantasizing them to fill a void. All these years, I didn't realize that I was so empty. Materialistic things do sometimes distract you from the things that matter – the priceless things, the things that you'll always remember, the things that make a difference in your happiness. Materialistic happiness was temporary. The more I thought about it, the more I was against Justin being a temporary high. He was fresh, something new, and he gave me hope for some reason. But I was also very naïve and vulnerable at this present time and I had no idea what his intentions were with me. He was a bit older and I was more inexperienced, but I wanted him, just like I wanted Clay. I wanted him more than Clay. I was overthinking and working myself up so much I forgot to wash my body. I just stood in the shower, soaking up the hot water. I began to wash myself with the hotel soap forgetting that I didn't have a scarf or any of my hair products. My hair got wet and I just decided to shampoo it since it was already reverting to its natural curls. My wild thoughts went back into hiding as I rinsed the soap and shampoo off. I was clean, fresh, and at ease. Tonight, would be a good night, I thought to myself, letting go of my insecurities and harsh reality as I stepped into the bedroom.

I heard the door open and close. I dropped my towel and stood in the mirror. There was noise in the living room, sounds of putting the pizza box on the desk table and opening plastic of some sort. I ignored it and stared at my reflection. Here I was with another man, hoping to fill a void. *If* I decided to lay it on him tonight and he never called again, then I could live with it. The night was still young, and I was prepared for the worst. Whatever happens, happens. I wanted to feel the love tonight especially after the incident at the party, even if it was just temporary.

—

I walked into the living room area covered in one of the robes that were hanging in the bathroom. He was already eating his pizza and watching TV.

"I ordered plain cheese. I forgot to ask you what you wanted and well, I don't have your phone number, so I couldn't call you. I hope that's alright."

Right he didn't have my number yet. Crazy how I was sitting in a hotel room with this man and we haven't even exchanged numbers yet.

"Cheese is fine. I don't really eat too much red meat and I don't eat pork at all, good call. Although, I love pineapples!" He stopped eating, letting his jaw drop.

"Crazy because I love pineapples on my pizza as well. Who would have ever thought you had good taste like me? Most people don't like pineapples on their pizza." I changed the subject back to the phone number situation.

"Give me your phone I'll put my number in. It wasn't intentional at all. I actually was getting ready to call you after leaving the party, I just happened to run into you before I had the chance." He handed me his phone and I entered my number. "There," I said, "now you can contact me whenever you like."

I walked over to the pizza box and picked up two pieces of pizza, grabbed a plastic cup and opened the bottle of cranberry juice. I loved cranberry juice. But I was puzzled at how he knew to get it for me.

"Have we met before?" He looked up away from his pizza at me in question.

"Have we met before?" He repeated.

"How did you know I liked cranberry juice?" He just looked at me with a blank expression.

"Well, I didn't but I bought a bottle of Grey Goose and I thought if you wanted some, you could use the cranberry juice as a chaser." I was so embarrassed. I'm sure if I was of lighter complexion I would have turned red.

"Right." I realized that I was overreacting. I needed to calm down, I was starting to jump off the bridge with some of the assumptions I was making. I poured my cranberry juice into the plastic cup and grabbed my pizza. I sat on the couch next to him and began to eat.

"Relax a bit. My intentions are pure." He said with a straight face. I wanted to argue, I wanted to tell him that every man in the world said that, even when they knew that their intentions were tainted.

"Shit! I have to book my flight. My phone is in the other room charging. Please remind me to book it before I go to bed."

"I can do that," he told me as he finished his pizza.

We sat and discussed what we wanted out of life, some short-term goals that we set for ourselves, and how we are going to achieve them. I fell in love with him, his mannerisms, the way he looked at me, his aura, and the way he smiled. I couldn't help but question all of this. Is this just temporary? Will I wake up tomorrow and forget all about him? Will the thought of him escape me once I got back home to face Dale? Better yet, will I even keep in touch with him once I get back home and continued to entertain Clayton? The feeling I get from him is real, but will it last? The way that I stared at him probably made him uncomfortable, but I was fascinated. I wanted to know more. I wanted to learn him in ways that conversation couldn't teach. At this point, I had no idea of what he was talking about anymore, I started to daydream about being intimate with him a long while ago. My pizza was gone, and the cranberry juice cup was empty. I stood up and dropped my robe.

"You're a wild girl," he said as he watched me walk closer to him, closely examining my naked body.

"I want to get closer to you." I lightly kissed him behind the ear while straddling him. I let my lips trail to his jawline and eased up to the bottom of his ear lobe, gently biting it. He tilted his head up in pleasure, letting out a light moan that I almost didn't even hear. Then he laid me on the couch and hovered over my body, still fully clothed.

"You sure this is what you want?"

I nodded my head yes and wrapped my legs around his waist. He moved them apart and picked me up, taking me into the bedroom.

"I don't want to make this awkward, but I would like to take a shower first if that's alright with you." It definitely made it awkward. I told him it was OK and that I understood. While he showered, I went ahead and booked my flight back home. I'd Uber my way to the airport at 11:00 in the morning. I didn't fly out of New York until 1:25 and would be home by 4:00 in the afternoon. Then I could shower and be at work by 6:00. I was still kind of pissed that Paisley went for Tommy's bullshit, but she does this frequently, so she should be fine. I'd check on her in the morning. I happened to glance at the side table next to the king-sized bed, seeing the $50 that I gave Justin for the pizza. He was so hardheaded. I put it back in my purse and waited in bed for him to finish his shower.

—

He stepped into the bedroom with his towel on, body screaming for attention. I quickly sat up and lifted the covers off me so that he could join, revealing my body to him again. It got a little cold in the bedroom while he was in the shower. He dropped his robe and flashed me his precious jewels. It was almost unreal. He was already hard as stone and ready to go. I had seen my fair share of penis', but none like his. It was like the perfect chocolate popsicle, the thick and long ones that you'd think about all day long on a hot and humid day. And when you finally got it, you wanted another one and another one and another. I didn't initially react, I let him get in bed and lie next to me before I began to make my sexual advances. The heat from his body sent chills through mine. He didn't even have to physically touch me, his energy alone made me weak and submissive.

"I don't want you to feel like I'm forcing anything on you," he said before turning to me and rubbing his fingers through my hair.

"Believe me, you aren't pressuring me to do anything. I came on to you. I want this. I just want to make sure I'm not pressuring you."

He laughed. "I really like you, everything about you is well balanced and I love that."

I wanted to tell him that he just met me and that the odds of him really liking me were slim. Maybe he enjoyed my company or liked the idea of me, that sounded more accurate. But I said nothing, I just let him play in my hair. If he wanted me too, then he could make the first move. He hovered over my body again, this time, his body as bare as mine. He began to kiss me from my mouth, to my neck, to my chest, to my stomach, to my hips on down to my toes. He even massaged my feet as he sucked them lightly. I moaned, loudly and freely. It felt incredible. He opened my legs again, but this time he stuck his head between them. He began to kiss my flower passionately and slowly. French kissing on my clit, his beard tickled my lips down below. He made his way closer to my ass, penetrating it with his tongue. I went wild. He was pregaming my body and it had me in nonstop pleasure. Once he let up off tongue kissing my vagina, I tried to match him, but he pushed me back on my back and told me that it was about me and my pleasure tonight. He kissed me, and I began to suck on his tongue as he made his way into my pussy. God, a thrusting burst of pleasure and bliss rushed through my body. I felt it all over, even in my toes as they began to curl. He slowly stroked and passionately went deeper and deeper inside me, forcing me to call out sweet nothings. We held hands and connected beyond the physical. He flipped me over and grabbed my lower back to arch it. As soon as he slid back inside me, I began to throw it back until I started to uncontrollably shake and scream in pleasure. He then began to speed up his stroke and go even deeper. I was creaming everywhere, and he was soaking it all up like the sun's rays on a hot summer day. Right before he climaxed, I lost feeling in my legs and almost collapsed. He held my body up and pulled out right before he sprayed my ass and back. I fell to the bed, face down and just laid there. I had never in my life experienced sex in raw form like that. I was instantly ready to go to bed. He got up and wiped the cum off my backside, wiped himself, and threw the wet towel in the bathroom. The damp spot from the wet towel became cool and soothing on my body. I fell asleep to him playing in my hair and whispering in my ear, dreaming of sweet tropical islands with white sand.

CHAPTER SIXTEEN

The sun flowed in through the windows of the hotel as I snuck out while he was still sleeping. I couldn't help but continuously glance at him as I put my clothes back on. He was so cute, soft, and his skin so warm and fluorescent. I kissed his cheek and whispered that I'd call him when I touched down. He was still half asleep, so he nodded and said OK. I'm sure once he woke up, he wouldn't even remember that. I was just appreciative of him still being next to me when I woke up. I was used to waking up in an empty bed.

My flight was quick and relaxing. I had the time of my life last night and it showed on my face, I was smiling from ear to ear. I was still having mini orgasms at the thought of Justin. I didn't even mind that the kid behind me was kicking the shit out of the back of my chair. I was so warm inside that I wasn't bothered by the ongoing cold air coming through the vents the entire flight. I was truly unbothered, and I wanted to stay this way.

As I unpacked my purse when I got home to switch bags for work, I noticed an envelope with cursive writing that said my name. It was sealed shut and unfamiliar at first glance. I opened the envelope and found a wad of cash. I counted out $3,000 in an assortment of bills and came across a note at the bottom of the bag that read: "For your valuable time, I hope to see you again." I was in utter disbelief. Justin hadn't texted me yet, so I pulled out my phone and typed in the number on his business card. I wanted to call, but I was really cutting close with me having to be at work in 30 minutes. I texted him letting him know it was me and that I was home, forgetting I saved my own number in his phone last night. I told him I was on the way to work and thanked him for the money and the fabulous night. After more thought, I sent another message asking him why he was paying me. I didn't get it, and I was starting to think that he either was an incredible flexor or he did a little more than flip houses and own properties.

I looked up the price of the room and hotel that we stayed at and reassured myself that the amount of money he was spending on just one night was too much. This man was crazy. He had to do something else on the side because this wasn't adding up. Either that or he was just willing to blow money on me which wasn't smart at all. He didn't really strike me as the flexing type, so my instinct led me to believe that he was doing something else that he didn't tell me. But it wasn't my business, he wasn't my man. Hell, I just met him yesterday.

My condo was empty per usual. Dale's suburban wasn't in the front and to my surprise it was spotless inside. He must have come home and cleaned while I was gone because before I left, my clothes were all over the bed and floor and the rest of the house was messy from my emotionally driven laziness. I had 10 unread messages that I didn't check, even before sending that message to Justin. I didn't have time, I'd be late for work. I'd check them there. My phone dinged three times, but I had no time to check that either, I just ran into the shower to hurry and get dressed so that I could make it just in time for work. I had no time to go into deep thought. I wanted to be alone and think, but I had to handle business. Maybe Justin would respect me or maybe he would assume I didn't value myself for letting him fuck the first night. We had a common interest and understanding as far as that was concerned, but I understand why he would judge me. As a man, I can see why he'd think I had a lack of respect for myself. I didn't know him at all, but I shared myself with him intimately. Maybe that's why he paid me. Maybe he felt sorry for me.

—

As I pulled into the office lot I scanned the cars outside of the building. Clayton's mustang was nowhere in sight. Tisa's office wasn't in an office building, it was more like a small ranch style home with business furniture and desks. It sat between two office buildings, so there were always excess vehicles in the lot since we shared it with all the employers of both buildings. As I walked in the door and up to my desk to set my bags down, I heard Clayton's voice. That's odd, I didn't see his car. I'd go talk to him once I got settled in. I was literally right on time and had so much to do.

The flashbacks of last night flooded my mind and I became warm inside. It was such a weird feeling. Almost how I felt when I used to be fresh in love with Dale. I quickly dismissed the feeling and sat down, plugging my charger into the wall and opening my binder.

"What does it take for you to return my texts?" Clayton was walking over to my desk.

"Good evening, how are you? I'm great! Thanks for asking," I said sarcastically, not looking up from organizing my desk. He became silent, so I stopped what I was doing to make eye contact. "I'm a busy woman Clay. I had to fly to New York yesterday to handle some business. In between naps and trying to get here on time, I haven't even had time to check my messages. I can show you if you'd like." I pulled up my message icon on my phone attempting to show him the number of unread messages that remained unopened in my inbox. He pushed my phone back in my direction, looking away from it.

"There won't be a need for that. I believe you. Once you check your messages, come to my desk and we can talk." He had a little sorrow in his voice. As he walked away, I got up and headed to Tisa's office. I hadn't seen her, so I needed to speak before I got into my work. I knocked on her door and she told me to come on in.

"Hey, just letting you know that I was here," I said as I put a stack of paperwork on her desk.

"I see. You seem extremely happy today. I can hear it in your voice. What's got you in these great spirits? Do tell." I really wasn't on her nosey ass shit today, so I kept it simple.

"Yeah, just appreciating life right now, nothing major. Hey, do you know a Robert Jackson? I met his nephew Justin yesterday at a rooftop event in Manhattan. He told me to send you his warmest regards." Her smile quickly faded. She walked around me to close the door.

"Sit down," she said as she put her pointer finger over her lips, motioning for me to keep quiet. She did this like we had a full staff of employees. Clayton was the only other employee excluding the janitor, and Janae the part time interior designer. I was confused, but whatever this was about couldn't be good.

"Did I say something wrong? What's going on?" She ignored my question and sat down next to me in one of her guest chairs and almost whispered.

"What did you tell him?"

Now shit was becoming sketchy.

"Who? Justin? I didn't meet Robert."

She put her hand over her forehead as if she was stressing.

"What did you tell him!?" She began to shout.

"I didn't tell him anything. I met him at the party, we got to talking, and he asked me what I did so I told him that I was an intern for you." She just shook her head continuously. "What's going on Tisa?" She was saying absolutely nothing.

"You have to cut all ties with Justin, Noel. He's not who you think he is." She stared into my soul, that's how serious she was.

"What do you mean? You aren't saying anything." I just sat in confusion. Tisa came closer to me and looked at the door as if she was checking the other side to see if anyone was listening.

"Robert and I were once married. He took Justin in as a young boy because his sister couldn't take care of him. But see, Robert is one of the most feared men in New York. Once I realized what he was doing…"

I interrupted her. "What do you mean what he was doing?"

She rolled her eyes at me. "Hush dammit. If you would just listen. This man has sold more dope than any nigga I know. Killed more people than the people in those gangster movies. He's not to be played with. And Justin isn't either. He's next up if something ever happens to Robert. He's his right-hand man and his shooter. It's in his blood. I don't want you to become victim to their actions. You're way too pure. I saw a lot of things when I was with Robert, a lot of those things I didn't want to see. Listen to me, please. Get out while you can."

I just sat in disbelief. I knew there was something else going on with Justin. I wish I wasn't right, because I really liked him. It was still fresh. I literally just met this man yesterday and the following day I'm finding out his dirty secrets. This shit is wild. I felt like I was being pranked. Just when I thought I met someone that I would be able to build with, I find out that he's not really in my best interest.

"Rob still won't sign the divorce papers, to this day. He thinks I belong in that type of lifestyle because of my leadership and skill. He had so many mistresses, I just couldn't take it. So, I made him leave permanently and I haven't seen him since. Every so often he will send me flowers and gifts and try to win me back. I was so young and stupid." She began to cry silently. All of this was just weird. Here I sat in my boss' office watching her cry over a man whose nephew I was very interested in. In the three years I've been working for her, I've never seen Tisa cry. I wanted to know why she was so emotional when it came to him. I didn't understand. I've seen her talk about bad breakups before, but none like this. I wanted to know more but this was a sensitive subject and I didn't want to intrude into her personal business.

"Did you say you made him leave? He lived with you? Here?"

She stopped crying enough to respond to me.

"Yes. Him and Justin used to come and live with me for months and go back and forth to New York when he wanted to get away."

I tilted my head and became irate. He bold-face lied to me.

"He told me he had never been here," I said with anger in my eyes.

She just shook her head. "He's been here more than a few times, Noel. He's a loose cannon. You didn't know though. Look, I can't tell you who to deal with, but I will say if you continue on with him to watch your back and surroundings. I don't want to hear about you getting into a bad situation because of his street beef. He's a nice young man, don't get me wrong, but it's too much baggage." She wiped her face and got up to sit in her chair. She didn't have to tell me to leave, I could tell by the look on her face she needed alone time. Her face was red, and eyes were puffy. I dismissed myself and sat back at my desk in amazement.

In deep thought, I sat for a while then remembered that I had a lot of work to do. I began pulling up emails and trying to read through them, but this was very heavy on my mind. I wanted to say something about it. I wanted to call him out on his lies, but one thing that Tisa taught me was to never act from emotion. If I was to text him right now, I would be acting off anger, so I decided against it. I didn't even know if this would continue, so why dig myself into a hole?

I pulled out my phone and began to read my messages. My mother texted me to check and see how I was doing then chewed me out because I haven't called her. Dale texted me and asked if we could talk. Justin texted me in response to him giving me money. He just sent me a kissing face and told me that I deserved it. And I did deserve it, but now I had to figure out what I was going to do about him. I texted my mom back and told her I'd visit this weekend and told Dale we could talk tonight once I got off work. I couldn't just keep avoiding him. There was a message from Paisley asking if we could talk over dinner tomorrow. I told her that was fine, and I would meet her at her place of choice. I finally got to Clayton's messages. He wanted to take me out Friday. I walked over to his desk and leaned over it.

"Yes, we can go out Friday. I'm free."

He instantly began smiling. "I hope you don't mind, I asked Tisa what your size was. I have a surprise for you. We're going to a ball. I'll pick you up around 7:00."

I was shocked that he took the initiative to get me something to wear. The only reason Tisa even knew my size was because we had an event we had to do to and I had to be measured thoroughly for a gown.

"I told you not to worry about it," I scolded him.

"What's it going to take for you to realize I'm going to do what I want? If I want to buy you a dress, I'm going to buy you a dress. Just be ready at 7:00, OK Noel? The extra mouth is uncalled for." I laughed and agreed.

Walking back to my desk, I took one more glance at him before I sat down. He was sweet, but I still wanted to know why he was pressing me so hard. I guess I'd enjoy the ride. It will come out eventually, I assured myself.

CHAPTER SEVENTEEN

It wasn't until I got home that the fact that Clayton's car wasn't in the lot at work started to bother me again. I was so damn distracted by Tisa and the whole Justin and Robert situation that I didn't even have time to be think about that minor detail. I wasn't going to say anything, but I was curious as to why he wasn't driving. I didn't know much about him, so it made me wonder; what if he had a girlfriend at home and he was driving her car this whole time? That could explain why he couldn't do breakfast that afternoon. I was thinking too hard on it. For all I know, he could just be having car troubles and could have taken an Uber to work. It was my fault that I ended up in these situations. I was constantly left wondering. Why? Because I barely knew these men that I decided to sleep with. I don't know what suddenly came over me.

—

I was waiting on Dale to come in the house so that we could talk. I needed to get this over with and fast. I was already starting to detach myself from him and I didn't need him to suck me back in with his profession of love and apologies. As I changed out of my clothes and into my pajamas, I stumbled upon the letter he had wrote me that I sat aside the night that Clayton was here. I decided that I wouldn't read the letter. I just feel like if I did, it would bring out subconscious emotions and I was really training myself to detach from him. I needed to stay on track. So, I kept the letter folded and put it back on the dresser.

I had so many things running through my mind. Let's start off by saying that the reason that I never repeatedly said anything about Dale having another woman is because I was brought up to know that once I ask about another woman, I became the other woman. Reflecting on that, I guess it didn't really matter because at the end of the day, I still am the other woman. This man had a whole child and secret relationship on me. Hell, maybe *I* was the secret relationship. I wasn't his girlfriend and he had to love her too. I was the other woman. I have no interest whatsoever in taking him back because he wasn't mine to begin with. I mentally left this relationship long before this incident. All the nights he would go missing without explanation, the days he'd come home late, the times where he'd buy me random gifts. I knew there was something going on. I knew that there was someone else in the picture. Granted, I had the wrong girl, but I knew that there was someone else. Shit, there's probably more than just me and her. Let's be honest, I had a feeling about Trinitee and I'll bet my last dollar that I'm right about that too. I just don't even care to know right now. I just want to know how we are going to situate this living situation. He might as well pack up and go because there is no way that I want him living with me knowing he has a second home to go to. He's not going to freely jump between me and her.

All this shit was weighing on my mind. I haven't even been focused on my work lately. I needed to set a day aside and work on *my* work. I felt reckless. I was certainly a loose cannon at this moment in time. I needed to be alone in the comfort of myself and my own energy. At this rate, I would have a nervous breakdown for sure. I felt like everyone was against me. Clayton probably had another life behind closed doors, Tisa was clearly withholding information about the Jackson family, Paisley just basically left me for dead in a completely different city and was misleading me the entire time I was there, and Justin lied dead to my face and then made fucking love to me an hour later. Oh, and turns out he's a goddamn murderer slash drug dealer. Then there's Dale. The worst has already happened with him. I just no longer want to see his face. I was literally going to explode if I didn't get any time alone to just breathe. I need that time very soon, or everyone was going to get the worst side of me. I wanted to break down in tears. I was frustrated and hurt for so many various reasons. I tried so hard, I did well in school, and I tried to remain focused. I just don't understand why this was all happening to *me* out of all people. What have I done to deserve all of this? My life was in shambles and I didn't know where to go, what to do, or who to turn to. I was lost, I was alone, and engulfed in all the temporary forevers'.

—

What the hell was taking Dale so long? I had texted him once I was on my way home from work letting him know that I was in route, and here I am an hour later at home waiting on him. I needed to speak with him, but I was so tired. I know I'd fall asleep soon if he didn't show. This was something he did often. He took his time coming to me in serious situations. It was all a part of his tactic of control and power. He knew I would wait on him, and that just showed him that I still cared. It gave him false hope. It made him feel like he still had an advantage over me and that there was a small chance I'd take him back. He'd be dismayed when he realized that is the furthest from the truth. The *only* reason that I was staying up is because I needed closure regarding this living situation. I needed to know if I should pack up and leave, or if he was going to give me the condo as a part of my pain and suffering expenses. After we came to an agreement on that, mutual or not, we no longer needed to keep in contact.

Over the years I always found a reason to hold on to him, and to not leave him. Now it didn't matter at all where this relationship went. I was no longer his, and he was never mine to begin with. The moment I gave interest to another man is when he officially lost me.

I grew irritable and tired of waiting on him. I tried calling him but there was no answer, as usual. He could come as late as he wanted to but as soon as I got out of the shower and put my body underneath those sheets, it was lights out. I wasn't going to talk in the morning. If he didn't catch me right after I got out of the shower, then it was a wrap. I was tired – mentally, physically, spiritually, and emotionally. I needed rest.

I grabbed a towel and washcloth out of the hallway closet and walked into the bathroom where I began to strip. Stepping out of my pencil skirt and thong, I turned towards the mirror on the back of the door. My skin was smooth, my legs the color of liquid chocolate, and my precious flower the color of butterscotch, nude and hairless. I unbuttoned my blouse and unhooked my bra. Glancing at my breasts, they resembled small melons. Not too big and not too small, just the right size for the perfect man. I was really turning into somebody I wasn't familiar with and it scared me. I was so carefree and rebellious now, I didn't know what I was capable of. I took my hair out of the top knot bun and let it hang, brushing against my back and ears. Glancing one more time in the mirror, I decided that it was time for me to get in the shower. I waited long enough. I always kept my phone on silent, so even if Dale would have returned my call, I certainly wouldn't have heard it. He had a key, he would be fine getting in the house.

This shower wasn't as long as it usually was. My mind wandered, but not too much tonight. I was growing more numb to the situation by the second. Sometimes I would feel like crying but to my surprise, I wouldn't form a tear. I wanted to release the pain, and I feel like crying would help me do that. It was a mind thing, shedding tears would have me a little at ease.

As the water covered my body and I cleansed myself, my eyes remained closed. My imagination ran wild. There were various colors and feelings moving throughout my body;

sounds of harsh waves against sand crashing into buildings and quickly moving back into the ocean. Once I was done showering I had to smell myself and make sure I cleaned every bit of me. I was so distracted, I forgot what I had washed. I don't even remember washing my hair, but it was wet, smelling of fresh coconut, and felt clean so I knew I had shampooed and conditioned it. I took a deep breath and dried my body, dropping the towel in the bathroom, walking nude into my bedroom. I literally felt as if I was walking on air. My steps were light, I didn't even feel the carpet between my toes. I sat on the bed and checked my phone, no response from Dale and from the looks of things, he wasn't here. I turned down my bed and got underneath the covers. I closed my eyes and drifted off to sleep.

CHAPTER EIGHTEEN

I felt a wisp of cool air cover my body and opened my eyes. There was Dale on the side of me, half naked and asleep. I rolled my eyes in the dim light that I left on.

"Seriously?" I tapped on his shoulder repetitively. "Wake your ass up!" I screamed. Then he finally opened his eyes. He looked hurt, but I didn't care. Why the fuck would he think I would be OK with him lying next to me like nothing ever happened. "Get up! Shit!" I got out of bed and stormed toward the bathroom. I went and used the restroom, giving him time to get clothed and get the hell out. Once finished, I walked back in the bedroom and he was still in the same position, the only difference is that he was awake.

"Noel, can we talk?"

I stopped dead in my tracks. "Can we talk? We were supposed to talk hours ago, and honey you weren't here. It doesn't work like that no more. You can't just show up and expect me to do what the fuck you say. All I need to hear is where you are going to be living from this day forward. If you plan on staying here, then I'm leaving!" I pulled the covers off him and wrapped up in them.

"Babe, I..."

I shook my head cutting him off. "There's no babe here. She don't live here anymore. Sorry! Are you staying or going?"

He leaned over and started to kiss me. "You can have everything, I just want to be with you this last time."

I laughed hysterically. Then thought about what he was doing. I didn't even care at this point. I used to be afraid that if I slept with him again, I'd fall in love just like I was before. *Nope*! The last time we had sex, I didn't feel anything. No form of connection whatsoever. That's why I know it would make no difference, so I let him have his way with me. Whatever would make him leave me alone in the future. OK, so if I slept with him, then he would go back to his happy family. That's all he needed was to think that he still had me wrapped around his finger, so he could go back to doing what he did best, living a double life. Then once he realized I wasn't on his shit, there would be nothing that he could do. I'd fuck, he'd leave, I'd sleep peacefully and so would he, with his newborn and his girlfriend. I'd be alone, but I'd rather be alone than suffocating in fake love all night. Yeah, I'll let him touch me this last time then no more. I sounded so stupid trying to convince myself that if we had sex I'd be OK. It wasn't that I thought I'd still be in love with him afterward, because I knew no matter what happened I still loved Dale. It would take some time for me to stop loving him. He's all I know, he's what I'm used to. I can't just forget about him tomorrow. Although I want to so bad, it just wouldn't happen that way.

—

I didn't say a word. I just opened the covers, welcoming him onto my bare body. A kiss here and there, we kissed so passionately, exactly how we did when I first fell in love. Just a few seconds ago, I was so sure that I would be OK doing this and now I'm second guessing myself. But it felt so good I didn't want to stop. My body was warm and filled with butterflies. There was a feeling in my chest that was indescribable, and my flower was filled with such excitement. But I knew that when this was over he would go back to where he's been sneaking off to for nine months. I was sick, disgusted, and overwhelmed with love. I broke my lips from his.

"What if I don't want to share you anymore?" I whispered then began to cry silently, looking in his eyes.

"Noel, you won't have to share me. I love you. I fucked up," he said in between kisses. I couldn't kiss him back, I just let him kiss me and bite my bottom lip. I just stared into space while he prepared to pleasure me. "I fucked up baby, but I love you. I'll always love you, let me make things right."

He uncovered my naked body and rested his head between my thighs. Suddenly those tears of pain and hurt turned into subtle tears from pleasure. I felt a rush climb through my body as soon as his tongue tickled my clit. I cried out and closed my eyes. Every twirl of his tongue painted a vivid picture in my mind. I was being hypnotized. He cupped my ass firmly while sucking my clit and licking down my lips, forcing his tongue into my hole. I was soft, and he was firm. He held me, so close, so tight, I fell weak at the knees and became one with my liquid form, taking to every curve he had within him. I let him win, over and over. Three deep breaths and his spaceship thrust off into my galaxy. He painted pictures inside of me, new constellations, and shook up my milky way. He pulled me out of the dark hole I was lost in. He let the different galaxies inside me pull him in different directions until he gravitated back to earth. This was more than sex, it was a spiritual experience. An out of body experience. This was us finally becoming one. It may have been too late now. He made sweet and genuine love to me like he'd never done before. It felt so good that I could only mouth what I wanted to say. I was quiet and at a loss for words. I almost forgot to breathe. This was better than any night with Clayton and couldn't be compared to the night I shared with Justin. I didn't want it to end. Chills were sent throughout my body, a quick cold breeze brushed past my nipples and I erupted uncontrollably. I held on to him as he went faster and deeper, my flower fell and became water and my grasp around him tighter. My juices spilled out on the sheets while his core became too heavy and collapsed. His explosion created a supernova inside of me. Fatigued, tired, and now no longer turned on, I moved from under him and went into my bathroom. I was so warm before and enjoyed the way he made me feel, but now my body grew cold and lifeless. I wiped myself, flushed the toilet, and washed my hands as I looked in the mirror. I was bored and disappointed. This new-found love for sex was ruining me. I can't control myself. I was being tossed around like a fucking salad damn near every week. The feeling didn't even last. This was a waste of my pussy and a waste of my time. He had to go, I had to be alone.

I walked out of the bathroom and grabbed the covers from around him, leaving his body cold and in the open, interrupting his sleep.

"Get out!" I screamed. His face covered in confusion, he tried to ask me what was wrong. "Get the fuck out! Get out of my life!" I dropped to the floor, crying gasping for air and curling my body into a fetal position. He didn't try to hug and cuddle then, he didn't kiss and reassure me, he got up and did as I asked. I was hurt but I asked for this. I knew how this would end and I slapped myself in the face expecting him to stick around and try after he got what he wanted.

"I'm not going to keep trying to work things out with you if you don't want me here," he said.

"Oh yeah, you weren't thinking like that before you got some pussy. Get the fuck on!" I couldn't help but cry. I stroked his ego and he left me there again.

"I try to comfort you and to make you feel good, as a man I want to make things right. You don't want me here, you don't want to be a family, and you don't want to forgive."

I was so damn pissed, I didn't even want to argue.

"A *family*?! *Forgiveness*?! Why in the hell would I even think about that shit?" I picked up the closest thing to me which happened to be a glass cup on my nightstand, and threw it at him. It hit the wall and shattered. "Fuck your family! Fuck your forgiveness! Fuck you, you manipulating ass bitch!"

He quickly zipped up his pants and walked out of what used to be our room. I was falling apart. I couldn't think. The tears wouldn't stop flowing and the anger that was nestled deep inside my body would not leave. I was shaking uncontrollably and overwhelmed with emotion. I got myself up and laid in the bed, wrapping myself in my comforter. There was no way I lost my shit like that in less than two seconds. I didn't even know myself anymore. Is this what love brought out of us women? This is what heartbreak made me become. I wouldn't wish this on my worst enemy. I stared at the wall until my eyes shut and I drifted involuntarily to sleep. I had to get my life together, and fast.

CHAPTER NINETEEN

I woke up to the sun shining on my face. My head ached, and my forehead was stiff and swollen from crying so hard. The shattered glass was still on my carpet, spread out to the corner of the room closest to the door. I couldn't think straight. I let Dale take advantage of me last night and ultimately, I played myself. How foolish of me to think that that would work in my favor. Now, I'm laying here full of cum and empty inside. I had to meet up with Paisley and talk to her, I think that I've put it off for too long. I honestly feel like what she did was dead wrong, and she didn't see the issue with it. I get that we are grown, and we can fend for ourselves, but she didn't mention a non-disclosure and she knows how I feel about that type of shit. Not only that, she pretty much left me out in NYC by myself. I know she wanted her money but damn, I was her best friend. I would have never left her in that situation. I had to remember that everyone is not like me, so in certain situations what was unacceptable in my eyes may be perfectly fine in someone else's.

I picked up my phone and called her. She agreed to meet me at IHOP in Oakley. I had a taste for some strawberry New York cheesecake pancakes and coffee. Ironic right? I carefully stepped around the broken glass into the bathroom to shower. I sat on the toilet once more trying to piss out any remaining venom Dale dropped off inside of me. I began to cry. I'm so stupid!

This shower unlike others was quick. I cleansed, rinsed, and dried my body. I didn't waste time daydreaming, crying, or feeling sorry for myself. I didn't reflect on the night before. My mind was blank. It was almost scary.

—

I'm not sure how this lunch meeting was going to go, but I didn't even care at this point. I was hungry as fuck I was going to say what I had to say and hear her out. If we could work things out that was fine, but if not, that's fine too. I felt how I felt about the situation and I'm sure she had her own feelings about it too. We were either going to agree to disagree or just say fuck the whole ass friendship. Either way, I was sick and more than tired of trying to save relationships. If it wasn't meant to be then it wasn't meant to be and that's all there is to it.

While putting my clothes on, I began to reflect on the years I put up with Dale's shit. I put up with his cheating and lying, his coming home late, him breaking my heart repeatedly and realized that if I turned my back on my friend after one fall out, I'd be the biggest hypocrite walking. No, I won't be like the rest of these women that let their man walk all over them but won't leave him no matter what he did, but in the same breath turn their back on their friend. The friend that came through when I cried over the same man that I took back umpteen times. Nah, I wasn't going to do it. I had to readjust my mind and be realistic.

I didn't bother applying makeup today, I just wasn't feeling it. Only thing I didn't want to show were the bags underneath my eyes and the puffiness in my face, so I grabbed a pair of sunglasses off my vanity and headed downstairs, stepping around the glass shattered on my carpet. I'd get it up later when I took the time out for myself.

Each room I walked past had me drifting in memories of Dale. I tried to stuff them back into a dark part of my mind where I didn't have to think about them just yet. I knew I couldn't erase them, but I had to keep my mind off the memories in the meantime, or I'd be a wreck. I truly was a wreck but publicly I hid it very well. I didn't want anyone to realize that I was hanging on by a thin strand. It was embarrassing. I was the woman who needed for nothing, my life was together, and no one would ever imagine me going through these hood rat things.

As I walked toward the door, I saw a plastic Walgreens bag on the table. I walked over and looked to see what it was. *Wow!* An emergency contraceptive with a note that said, "I know you haven't been taking your birth control for quite some time now, so I thought I would help you out." He was such an asshole. I don't care how good the sex was last night, he yet again shitted on my very existence. He didn't give his new girlfriend a Plan B pill, obviously. But I was the one that he made sure wouldn't get pregnant. Another slap in the face!

I sat the bag back on the table and headed to my car. I didn't want a child at all, but this was a hard pill to swallow. Literally. He had a child on me, a whole separate relationship so carelessly. He begged me to work things out and now that I let him dip and slide in, he made sure that I wouldn't get pregnant. Crazy how in a month's time, things could change so drastically. Just a month ago, he didn't care if I was pregnant or not. He didn't give me a Plan B then. He didn't even ask me if I came on like he usually did. He didn't care so why should I? Hell, I seriously thought about not taking the pill just to be petty and get his feathers ruffled up. But that would only do damage to me ultimately. He didn't have to stick around. And I would be shattered if he decided to bail on me. You never really know a person until you're put in a serious situation. Then I'd be left with a bill for an abortion or worse, with a child that I'd have to take care of all alone. It wasn't worth it, I couldn't take the chance.

Grabbing my purse off the dining room table, I remembered that the money Justin gave me was still in the envelope waiting to be deposited in the bank. Dale and I had a joint account. I never took the time to create my own account, so I had to make time today to deposit this money. Actually, I think I'll take a different route. I was going to buy a safe and stash it in the house. This wasn't legal money and I knew nothing of how to cover up dirty money in the banking system. If I was going to deal with Justin, then I may as well get a safe. I was very indecisive about him, because you can't always believe what other people tell you. Although Tisa seemed sincere, she could very well be trying to sabotage what him and I shared. After all, she wanted me with Clayton and that was no secret. I didn't have that many options. I was used to being taken care of, so I had to either continue to fuck with Justin, or cut all ties with him and somehow take control of my life, and quick.

I got to stay in the condo and Dale was going to continue to pay. He paid my Tahoe off in cash so as far as those two things, I was straight. But I needed to seriously better myself and come up. At any given moment Dale, could revoke on these things. I would be out here stranded or worse, forced to move back with my mother who lived more than an hour away. I loved my job and it was going to help my career in the long run. I wasn't trying to backtrack or move, so I needed a backup plan and emergency money. $3,000 was a good start, but I needed more. I just had to plan ahead. I refused to be ass out. So, I grabbed my purse and headed out the door. Today would be interesting. I had to prepare myself, both mentally and emotionally. I would handle it though, I always did.

CHAPTER TWENTY

As I walked into IHOP and sat down at the table with Paisley, I began to think about how Clayton didn't drive to work the day before. Yet again, I began to wonder where his car was. I didn't understand why I was pressing the issue so damn hard, but it bothered me. It bothered me a lot. I was curious and felt as though there was something going on behind my back. I planned to ask him on our date Friday.

Paisley and I greeted each other and ordered our food. We both knew what we wanted so it was easy to get straight to the point. The table was silent until the waitress brought us back our drinks. I ordered unlimited coffee and Paisley ordered water. She squeezed her lemon at the rim of her glass as I opened and poured creamer in my mug. She was still silent, so I broke the ice.

"I just think that as a friend it was wrong to leave me in a new city all alone."

She sipped her straw.

"Well technically you weren't alone, Justin took good care of you. You're still in one piece." My mouth dropped. I can't believe she was being so insensitive.

"But I came with *you*." I raised my voice, becoming angry.

"Listen Noel, we are two grown ass women. I don't need to hold your hand like some stupid ass child. Even if you were by yourself, you had a phone and some money, you could have booked a hotel room all by yourself without supervision." She looked me dead in my eyes and didn't even blink. I just sipped my coffee.

"As your friend, I wouldn't have let you walk away and be alone in an unfamiliar city."

Paisley poked her bottom lip out and nodded, showing me that she understood but that she still didn't see what she did as wrong.

"Well, I apologize if I made you feel 'alone.' That wasn't my intent. I needed my money regardless of you keeping your word or not. I have bills to pay, and I no longer have a man in my corner to hand me everything."

This was not what I expected.

"It's feeling real shady over here Paisley. Care to elaborate on what's really going on?" I took off my sunglasses and laid them on the table. She spoke slowly and clearly.

"I, unlike you, don't have someone that'll foot the bill for me. I make my money how I make it. Therefore, one monkey doesn't stop the show. I wasn't going to leave just because you threw a temper tantrum and didn't want to be involved anymore. That's not my problem. My bills still have to be paid and if I have the opportunity to eat, then I'm going to eat, whether you want to sit at my table and dine with me or not."

There was no arguing with that. But I'd take my friendship over any amount of money, any day.

"See the difference between you and I, no dollar amount is worth my friendship. There's nothing left to be said here. I love you dearly, but I think it's best I love you from a distance," I told her while getting up from the table. "No hard feelings, we just have to agree to disagree. No beef, we just do things differently."

Paisley just shook her head. "I love you too," she said, still sitting at the table waiting for her food.

I placed the same $50 bill that I gave Justin to pay for the pizza down in front of her.

"It's on me, enjoy your meal. Until we meet again," I told her as I walked out. I may have overreacted, but I needed that practice. I needed to learn how to love people from a distance and walk out of their life. I didn't feel bad, I just put my sunglasses back on my face and thought of where I would eat. I was hungry, but I couldn't stay there and eat with her. I was pissed and hurt. In that moment, I vowed to myself that I wouldn't be weak again.

—

Luckily Walmart was around the corner. I checked my phone and had a missed call from Justin. I sent him a text telling him I was out running errands and I'd call him once settled in. I sent another text to my mom telling her I'd stop by sometime next week instead of this weekend because I was really backed up with work. I had two missed calls from Tisa, I figured she was more important, so I returned her call. No answer. I left a message telling her I was returning her call and wanted to see how she was doing. I didn't work until tomorrow, so I wouldn't see her face to face until then. I hesitantly called Clayton back.

"Hey babe, what are you doing?"

I chuckled and told him I was on the way to Walmart.

"OK, I'll make this short. Are you a silver or gold type of girl?"

I laughed because I knew he was up to something.

"I prefer gold, but I like both. Why do you ask my love?" I was nearing Walmart and hoped he would get to the point. I was a little more than irritated today.

"Just be ready at 7:00 on Friday." He quickly hung up. That was easy. It was Tuesday and still somewhat the beginning of the week. All that meant was the rest of my week was bound to go smooth because the beginning was so full of shit.

I walked into Walmart and picked out a cart. I had to buy groceries and other household things and figured I should probably do it now. Shopping alone was also a good time to reflect on my life. It was therapeutic in a sense, and I enjoyed it. The first thing I had to get was the safe. That was the entire reason for coming to Walmart. I knew if I didn't get it now that I would forget. So, I headed straight to the hardware department. I leaned over my cart and took out my phone. There was a text from Justin asking if I would be able to come back to New York soon. I asked how soon and ended the text with possibly. I was eager to go back because I needed money and if he was what Tisa said he was, then he would be able to help me. I didn't really think too hard on the danger I could possibly be putting myself in. I was so focused on making my current situation better than what it was.

I guess me texting and walking with a cart was the wrong idea. I felt my cart hit something and bounce back. Instantly, I was apologizing for my lack of attention to what I was doing.

"It's alright. I wasn't paying attention either."

I looked up at the woman I hit with my cart. She looked so familiar, but I couldn't figure out who she was. And then it hit me.

"Perez?" I asked.

"Yes ma'am. And you're Paisley's friend, right? Noel?"

I nodded. She looked relieved to see me.

"What brings you to Cincinnati?" I asked her, genuinely confused. A few days ago, we were just at her house in New York. She didn't mention coming to Cincinnati.

"Well actually, I'm here for an audition tomorrow. I don't know if you know or not, but I'm an actress. It's funny that I ran into you. I was just headed to Paisley's house to stay. You want to come out with us tonight?"

I quickly shut her down. "No that's OK, I have some work to do. But it was nice seeing you again." Say less, I thought to myself.

"Oh OK. Do you live close to her?"

"Not really. I'm about 15 to 20 minutes out of her way. I live in White Oak. It's behind Colerain Avenue, near Northgate mall."

"Well yes girl it was very nice seeing you again, I'll be sure to tell Paisley I saw you." She handed me her business card. I nodded and walked away.

That was weird and awkward as hell. I wonder why she was really here. Ever since Paisley started acting funny, I questioned everything. Poor little Perez had nothing to do with our dealings, but I just feel like she's guilty by association. What the fuck was she doing here? I had to ask myself the question once more. This shit is just really off to me. Then she gave me her business card like I asked for a service. Weird. Maybe she was just trying to promote herself. Who knows.

I picked up my safe, got a few groceries, and made my way out of Walmart as fast as possible. Something just wasn't right. I was starting to think I was crazy but shit just didn't make sense to me. I had a gut feeling something crazy was getting ready to happen. Whatever it was, I had a feeling it wouldn't be good.

CHAPTER TWENTY-ONE

I pulled into the driveway and saw Dale's suburban. What the *hell*!? Why is he here? I grabbed my bags out of the car and struggled to open the door. Once I got inside, I saw Dale sitting on the couch with a newborn baby.

"Oh, hell nah! What the fuck are you doing here? And why would you bring the baby?"

Dale shushed me, showing me that his daughter was asleep. Not to be rude, but I didn't really care.

"It's like a never-ending cycle with you," I said as I put the groceries on the table and walked toward him. "What do you want from me Dale? Honestly. We aren't a family, that's not my kid. Get the shit out of your head. We're over. Your daughter doesn't deserve this." She was so pretty. She had a head full of hair and was brown just like him. He ignored everything I said and introduced us.

"Noel, this is Journey." He tried to hand me the child. Oh no, as a woman I didn't even want to hold her. I'd be pissed if my daughter was getting handed over to my man's other woman.

"Does your girlfriend know you brought her here? Out of respect, I think I'll pass on holding her."

"I told her everything. She wants to meet you." I began to laugh. This had to be a joke.

"Is this some type of sick ass joke? Why would she want to meet me? And then what? This ain't no damn sister wives' situation. We aren't a family. There's no polygamy going on here." I was pissed, and it was written all over my face, in my actions, and deep in my tone.

"Could you just chill the fuck out for a second? Damn!"

"No, no I cannot. It's about time you leave. Can you leave the keys on the table please? Don't come back here. Tell your girlfriend that it's nothing personal, but I don't feel like there's a reason we should communicate. I'm not dealing with your shit anymore. I can't, and I won't."

Dale just sat rocking baby Journey in his arms.

"Um, hello!" I know he heard me. I'm sure the neighbors down the street heard me. I'm sure Paisley heard me all the way across town. He ignored me and shushed the child as if she were crying. I wasn't mad at her, I was angry at him. How could he create a whole separate life without even giving me a heads up? The man that I loved! Was I not worth a warning at least? Shit, if I would have known that he was in a separate relationship, I would have programed myself to let go and move on. Maybe I would have been well on my way by now. Maybe I would have been at peace. Maybe, just maybe.

He looked up at me then down at the couch, gesturing for me to sit. I shook my head no. He just stared blankly in my eyes.

"Please Noel, for Journey's sake. She deserves to know the woman I gave my heart to."

I just laughed. This wasn't for the baby. This wasn't for anyone's satisfaction but his. I was hurt, humiliated, broken, and overall, I was numb. I walked to the door and opened it.

"Please just see yourself out. Please. I won't ask you again." I stepped behind the door.

"I'm not leaving until you hold her," he said firmly.

I rolled my eyes. "Then I guess we'll just sit here all night because I'm not doing it." I didn't move a muscle. I literally had all night, so it didn't matter to me. I guess he had all night too because he didn't blink.

"Hmm suit yourself." I shut the door and walked upstairs to the bedroom. If he wanted to be petty and sit there the whole night, he could. But I wasn't even going to entertain it. I had paperwork to finish and phone calls to make. I pulled out my phone to text Clayton and an incoming call came in. It was Justin. I answered on the second ring.

"Hey babe." Hey babe? I had to laugh. I can't believe I called him babe. I began to fiddle with my clothes and drop them to my knees, continuing our conversation. He asked me to fly out next weekend for a visit. I was still a little ticked off about him lying to me. But I didn't lash out. All I ask for is honesty and if you don't have enough respect to be honest then it's pretty much over for you, but I'll play his game.

"I had a few words with Tisa today. She told me to give you all warm regards and told me to tell you that her door is always open if you need to come back and stay," I said dryly, putting my silk gown over my head. He giggled a little.

"I guess you caught me. Yes, I used to live in Cincinnati. I just wanted to see if you'd ask her about me. Nice to see that you care."

"Well, it's not that I care, I just want to know who I'm involved with. And please don't lie to me again. That's the quickest way out the door. Book the flight, I'll be there." I hung up the phone and scanned through my text messages. Nothing from Clayton. I opened a new message and told him that I couldn't wait to see him and thanked him for thinking to ask me to go out. I laid down and drifted off to sleep. My dreams were filled with freedom and easing of my pain. There,

I didn't hurt anymore. I was just floating in the air. Warmth took over my body and I became one.

CHAPTER TWENTY-TWO

I woke up in awe. This feeling I felt in my dream, I wanted to feel it again. If I could feel this way every night, I wouldn't deprive myself of sleep. I didn't want to wake up. I wanted to permanently be free. The birds were chirping, and the sun played peek a boo through my curtains. I was back on earth. I was numb again. I hated my life. Suddenly, I heard a baby crying. Are you fucking kidding me? I hopped out of bed and headed downstairs.

"Why the hell are you still here?" I shouted at Dale as he changed Journey's diaper. He just shushed me again. At this point I was tired of seeing his face. I was tired of being in his presence and breathing the same air. I grew sick to my stomach and felt every drop of my blood begin to boil. He took me out of my character. I was very mild tempered and calm, like water. Lately there was a side of me that I've never seen before. I was fire and I was hot, yet, I was cold and not present in my body. I was no longer in control of myself.

"Dale, can you *please* leave? I'm literally begging you to go. This situation isn't healthy. I don't want to be a part of your blended family. I want to move on in peace, by myself, all alone." He looked away from me, he appeared hurt and dismayed.

"Says the person that had another man in our bed a day after we broke up."

Understanding his sense of betrayal, I sarcastically chuckled and shook my head. I walked up to him and took Journey out of his arms, beginning to rock her from side to side.

"She doesn't deserve this," I said looking him in his eyes. Her eyes were so precious. They were filled will innocence and purity. Mixed emotions took over me. I knew that this child was such a blessing, even if she even though she didn't come from my womb. She was so beautiful and filled with so much life. Her powerful lively energy shot through me. My body was warm again, I felt free once more. She smiled at me. All I saw was her father. The sweet side of him, the side I rarely got to see. She will be a real charmer as she gets older. I gave her back to him. He smiled. Holding Journey in his right arm, he reached out to me with his left. I shook my head and turned to go back upstairs. His eyes burned deep holes through my gown, but I didn't turn and look at him. I did all that I could, now I had to move on with my day. Hopefully by the time I got dressed and ready to head out he'd be gone. If not, he could stay. I just wouldn't be here.

—

Today, Tisa was going to California to meet with a production company about a potential movie for spring. She never told us too many details until everything was set in stone and I couldn't blame her for it. While she was away it would just be me and Clayton at the office, which was more than fine with me. When I pulled into the parking lot, I saw Clayton's

Mustang; shiny and clean, parked neatly in front of the building. He was always early. To him, being early meant you were on time. Seeing his car just made me think about the day that I didn't notice it when I pulled into the office. Here I was again, probably overthinking the entire situation. But for some reason, that was sort of a red flag. I had to ask him about it, face to face, because if he was lying, I'd be able to tell immediately. So, I walked up to the building, heels clicking, my blazer swaying and attempted to open the door. It was locked. That's weird as fuck, the door was never locked when someone was inside. I began to look for my key, with listening ears. I was trying to eavesdrop and observe what was going on inside the office that shouldn't have been locked. It was dead silent.

"Hello?" I said as I walked into the office. There was no answer. I walked around to my desk and set my bags down. Looking up at Clayton's desk, his belongings were there but he wasn't. That was weird. I pulled my phone out of my purse and looked at my notifications. I was so horrible at texting it made me sick. I had 22 unread messages and I wasn't necessarily excited to read them. Looking over the messages I saw three from Clayton. I'm sure when I did see him, I'd get chewed out for that. Besides the fact that I already wasn't the best texter, there was a thousand and one things going on in my life right now that made texting my last priority.

"I wonder what it would take for you to respond to my messages," Clayton said turning the corner, breezing past my desk. I laughed and disregarded his comment.

"I said 'hello' and no one answered. I was on my way to look around, I thought I was going to walk in to a dead body or something. Don't scare me like that."

He sat down at his workstation, pulled out a portfolio, and sat it on his desk.

"You ready for our date?"

I paused. "I've been meaning to talk to you about that. I don't think I'm going to be able to go."

His smile faded, and he just looked at me with hurt in his eyes. "Are you going to tell me why?"

"I was joking, relax. I can't wait to go out and represent you." I smiled at him, but he didn't think my joke was funny. He just began to start his work. The silence made me realize how childish and immature my joke really was. I just wanted to see how he'd react. This man was serious about me. Not sure why, but he certainly was. I got up from my desk and took a seat on the corner of his. Grabbing his face, I tilted his chin up gracefully so that he was looking directly at me. He began to blush. It was adorable. His smile spread across his face and it made me feel warm inside. Not like the warmth I felt in my dream, but it was very similar to it.

"Hey, I'm sorry. Sometimes my sarcasm is a bit overbearing. But I'm honored to be your date Friday. Where are we even going? You never said and you're getting me dresses and jewelry. I'm eager to know."

Clayton then grabbed my face and gave me a kiss on the lips. That kiss turned into three and three became a whirlwind of neat wet kisses. His breath tasted like berries and cream. Mine probably tasted of coffee. I drank a cup on the ride here. I broke away from our long kiss. I was shocked that he was bold enough to do that while at work. I wasn't mad about it though, Tisa wasn't here. It just was the simple fact that we were in a professional setting that threw me off.

"Just kiss me like that while at work?"

"I want you to be mine, Noel. So that if I want to, I can kiss you wherever and whenever I want."

I just sat in shock. I like Clayton, but I liked Justin too. And I wasn't completely over Dale. He was moving too fast for me. I mean, I barely knew him. We work together but we've only been out a few times. I wasn't comfortable jumping into a relationship with a man that I barely knew. It's a scientific fact that it can take up to four years to truly get to know someone. We've been knowing one another for a few months. There was no way he really thought I'd be willing to jump head first into a relationship. I guess I was taking too long to respond or show any emotion, so he answered for me.

"I know it's soon. There is absolutely no pressure, but I just wanted to let you know that."

I still had a blank look on my face when a light bulb lit up in my head.

"Where was your car the other day?" You can tell I threw him off with that question.

"What do you mean?"

I explained to him that when I pulled up a few days ago his car wasn't parked in the lot, but he was here. I also took the initiative to explain that this question sparked out of curiosity. He looked to the left.

"I had to Uber to work because my car wouldn't start that morning. I was going to call you, but I didn't want to have you come all the way across town to swoop me up."

I nodded, indicating that I understood. He was lying, he looked to the left before he answered. That was a natural reaction that humans did right before they were about to lie. The confrontational part of me wanted to stop him dead in his shit. But I didn't, it was too soon. And since it was such a simple lie, I didn't want to seem like I was being extra. It was Wednesday. I'd see him again Friday for this date. Maybe I'll brush on it again Friday, so I won't seem so pressed about it. I got what I wanted though, an answer. It may not have been an honest one, but it was what I asked for.

I went back to my desk and did my work. Every so often I'd look up at him and catch eyes. He was handsome and charming, but I don't know about the lying. I wonder what else he was lying about. I guess all my questions couldn't be answered immediately. They'd come to the light eventually. I just had to be patient wait and see. What the hell as my issue? I was super pressed about what could possibly be wrong with this man. I was always in search of something. Dale did something to my mental. He fucked with my trust. The most perfect man right here in my face and all I could do was look for his flaws. My trust in men was diminishing fast. I should be enjoying our time together but instead, I'm in search of a deal breaker. Maybe it wasn't the men that had issues, maybe it was me. Either way, I was confused. That's something I couldn't ignore or let go of. I had to sit and figure me out. I was in no rush to move forward with any man.

CHAPTER TWENTY-THREE

I was so cold. My body was warm to the touch, but my mind was frost bitten, my heart was ice, and my love was nonexistent. I saw the individual raindrops hit my dashboard and suddenly felt faint. Dale's suburban was gone. I thought I'd be happy, but all I could think about was Journey. That could have been me. I could have had his child. Now let's disregard the fact that he would have had two newborns months apart in age. My mind went straight to the fact that if I would have remained pregnant and had the child, I would feel like I have a reason for living. I'd have someone to live for. I'd have someone to speak life into. I didn't feel like I had a purpose right now. I felt like I was just existing. I had a routine; everyday I'd get up and go to work or go out or do something to fill up my day to keep my mind off the sadness in my heart. I was physically present, but absent in my mind and spirit. So, what if I did have the baby? I wonder if I would have been like the rest of these women and kept dealing with my child's father off the strength of our history and our bloodline. That would have been equally as draining. Maybe I would have been cordial with him and been alone, just me and my child. I know for a fact I didn't need a child right now. I had to worry about my career and my work. But the way I was feeling made me second guess. I'm sure I'd wake up tomorrow feeling completely different after coming to my senses. My life was in shambles and I was seriously over it. There was this empty feeling that wouldn't go away. I needed to pray, I needed to heal, I needed to cry. Usually when you cry, you feel better. You feel a sense of relief. But I couldn't even get my eyes to water. So, there I sat silently listening to the rain fall in my truck. This was proof that materialistic things do not make you happy. They are temporary highs and distractions that make us feel better for the moment, but subconsciously we're still the same miserable people. Tahoe's' were my favorite SUVs and my dream car ever since a little girl but receiving it didn't heal the hole in my heart. No amount of money or materialistic gifts would be capable of fixing that.

I sat still in that car for an hour, just letting my thoughts run wild. There was no progress, I didn't feel better afterward. I felt the same. Stagnant. I was still lonely and confused. I wanted help, but I didn't really know what was wrong. I just knew that I was unhappy and couldn't seem to find my way to happiness. I couldn't get back in the groove of things. It pissed me off and it made me sad. I got out of the car and walked to the door of what was now my condo. I became dizzy as I grabbed for the door. I quickly caught my balance and pushed my weight on the door as I opened it. I hadn't eaten much today, that was most likely the reason for my lightheadedness. Looking in the direction of the kitchen I stopped and thought about what I could eat. There was one issue though; I had no appetite. Maybe I could find something light. Fruit and oatmeal sounded pretty good. But I had fruit but no oatmeal. Lately when I ate strawberries, my throat began to itch so I wanted to stay away from those. I looked in the refrigerator and found a cantaloupe that I almost forgot about. Picking it up and examining it to make sure that it wasn't old, I saw that it was still good. That was a great snack, it was light and filling. The salt, I almost forgot the salt. My grandmother used to sprinkle a little bit of salt on top of the cantaloupe after she cut it. It made it sweeter. I cut the cantaloupe in small squares, easy to bite. There was less mess, and it gave the impression of having more. And right now, more is all I needed. More love, more sincerity, more attention, more life. I sprinkled the salt over the bowl and plopped a piece in my mouth. It was cold and sweet and sent a rush through my body. Suddenly I was warm again. I smiled on my way up the steps. The appetite that I thought that I didn't have was now alive. I carried the bowl with me up the steps and into my bedroom. I sat my bowl on the edge of my bed as I gracefully stripped and threw my clothes in my laundry basket. I spun around like I was ice skating and almost lost my balance, knocking over my bowl. All my sweet cold cantaloupe hit the floor. There was silence. My sudden happiness turned to fury. My fury turned into sorrow. I fell to the floor with my cantaloupe and laid out on the carpet. Looking up at the ceiling, I began to wail. The tears that I was in search of hours ago finally began to fall. They wouldn't stop flowing and I almost couldn't breathe. I cried so hard my eyes began to burn, my head felt like pressure was going to make it burst, and my nose began to run down to the bottom of my top lip. I wiped my lip and my face and began to put the cantaloupe back in the bowl. I was falling apart. There was no self-control. What the fuck was wrong with me?

Suddenly I had the urge to do something crazy. I set the bowl down on my dresser and went into the bathroom. I went through the bathroom closet and drawers in a mad search until finally I found what I was looking for. I took my ponytail holder out of my hair and starred in the mirror. My face was puffy and slightly red. I took my clippers and plugged them in the outlet above the sink. The buzzing sound they made was music to my ears. I began to cut my naturally curly hair. Years of emotion and growth bounced off my bare body and fell onto the bathroom floor. There was hair everywhere and my hands were shaking. I abruptly dropped the clippers, they came out of the outlet and hit the floor, breaking into small pieces. I looked in the mirror one last time and headed to the shower, turning the lever as much to the left as I could without burning my skin off. I ran back into my room and grabbed my phone. I called Clayton. He answered on the second ring.

"Don't say anything, just come over," I ordered.

"OK, on my way."

I sent a follow up text and told him the door would be open and that I was hopping in the shower. I went and unlocked the door and stepped into the tub letting the hot water rain down on me. I let it cover my body and my new hair and sat directly under the flow of the shower head. I reached up and grabbed my shampoo and began to cleanse. I scrubbed so hard I thought I would have scabs in my scalp the next day. I wanted all the emotion, hurt, and pain out of my system. I wanted it gone tonight. I wanted to be at peace. I must have washed myself 10 times when I finally heard a knock at the bathroom door.

"Noel, I'm here."

I yelled out, "OK, I'll be out in a second." I quickly rinsed off, hopped out the shower, and dried off. I left my hair wet and let it drip down my neck. The bathroom was a mess and I didn't even care. I just wanted to feel love, even if it was temporary. I patted my hair dry with a towel and put it around my waist as I walked into my bedroom. Clayton was sitting on my bed waiting for me. His face lit up.

"You cut your hair?"

I nodded.

"I love it!" he said reaching for the bowl of cantaloupe.

"*No*! Don't eat that. I dropped them on the floor."

He put the bowl back on the dresser and laughed.

"Did you lock the door?" He responded yes as he took his shoes off and moved them to the side of the bed. I dropped my towel and grabbed him by the waist, sitting on top of him. I dove head first into kissing him. The kisses were wild. He ran his hands from my ass to my back. I undressed him and laid him on his back. He moaned lightly as I kissed and licked his stomach and teased his dick. We were both naked and ready. I made love to his manhood, running my tongue slowly around his bell head, swirling in circles, and slowly sucking and releasing while jacking off his shaft. I made sure to make it extra wet as I continued my routine. I think he may have been ready to come because he pushed me away and threw me on the bed, entering my walls. The kisses he planted on my chest made me whimper in pleasure. He grabbed my neck and started to stroke harder, then started to nibble on my left ear. My body went wild from pleasure.

"Fuck!" I cried out so loud, I'm sure the neighbors heard me two streets over. He turned me over and pounded me out until he came all over my back. We took deep breaths and let our heart beats slow down before he went and got a towel to clean me off. We laid in peace, side by side, until the sun woke me up in the morning.

CHAPTER TWENTY-FOUR

Tonight was the night Clayton and I were going on our first official outing. We have been out on a date before but not in public. He bought me a dress and some sort of accessory that I have yet to see. I was nervous. Yes, he had style, but when it comes to women, I wasn't so sure. What if I didn't like what he picked out for me? How do I tell him that I can't wear it? He didn't have to buy me anything. It's more to women's shopping than finding something cute and stylish. There's fit and comfort, there's body types and hair, you must keep all of that in mind when shopping for a woman. So yes, I was very nervous. He may have picked the dress out with my long natural hair in mind. I was now disgustingly close to having a fade. That was hyped, it wasn't that short, but it wasn't long at all. My hair was literally a short curly fro. I looked in the mirror and cried. All I could think was what have I done? I literally sat in the tub until the water turned ice cold and cried until there was no more liquid forming in my eyes. I felt so ugly and bare. I felt so empty, *still*. Even though Clayton loved it. Even though he made love to me the night before. I still felt ugly and none of my tactics to feel beautiful and loved again worked. I was shattered. There was a part of me that was so sure I'd get over this phase. Then another part of me wasn't sure if I'd ever feel like me again. The happy me I was before all this chaos transpired. But then again, I had to really think. Was I ever truly happy, or was I just happy enough to get by? The more I sat and thought about it, the more I realized that I was never truly 100 percent happy. I've never sat and thought about any of this until now. It was hard for me to even get out of bed in the morning. I used to do it so naturally, I had a reason to get up and go to work, I had my future in mind. Now it's like I don't care about where I go in life. I don't even want to wake up in the morning. If the good Lord wanted to call me home right now, I wouldn't put up a fight. I'd just go. I'd leave everything and everybody without saying goodbye.

I felt like no one cared about me and no one would miss me if I was gone. Nothing was important to me anymore. I was having sex with multiple men back to back, in different cities, on no birth control, taking no emergency contraceptives, and using no protection. It was clear that I didn't give a fuck about life. I could have easily contracted an STD or became pregnant without even knowing who the father would be. In a month's span, I became the total opposite of what I used to be. I was a whore in search of something I knew I would never find under the conditions I created for myself. Now, I was a bald-headed whore with no confidence. I didn't even think that I was pretty anymore. There were bags under my eyes and it looked as though the soul had been sucked out of me. I was lost, and I just couldn't see myself being found again.

—

It was 5:30 PM and I had just showered and shampooed my hair when I heard a knock at my door. Clayton told me that he'd be dropping off my dress and whatever other gift he got me around this time. I threw on some yoga pants and a big t-shirt to open the door. To my surprise Clayton wasn't who I met at the door. There was a limousine driver standing there, all suited up, with a piece of paper in his hand. He handed it to me and told me he'd be waiting in the limo. The paper was folded and crisp, it read, "Take a ride in the limo, he'll take you everywhere you need to go in preparation for tonight. I can't wait to see you." I smiled inside. Motioning that I'd be right back, I quickly ran and got my shoes, and grabbed my purse and my keys off the table. I shut the door and locked it on my way out and hopped inside the limousine. I had never had any one do something like this for me. It made me so happy that I wanted to cry. But I didn't. Everything was still in motion, and at any given moment something could fail or go wrong. I'd save my tears for something like that if it happened. I always expected the worst and for once I wanted to be shown that I didn't have to always think something bad would happen.

We pulled up to a hair salon in Silverton called Ladies First. The driver let the partition down and explained that this was my first stop of the night and he'd be waiting for me right outside when I was finished. I got out of the limo and walked into the salon. It was filled with life on this fine Friday evening. There were people in every chair, three barbers on the left side and two hair stylists on the right. Everyone greeted me with kindness and warmth and pointed toward the back of the shop. I walked through an open door to the back and saw three more chairs with stylists and clients. The one furthest to the back welcomed me to sit in his chair.

"You must be miss Noel."

I nodded and asked him his name.

"James. I've been cutting Clayton's hair for years. I used to work in a few shops but then decided to open my own and I've been successful ever since."

I could learn from him. I just wasn't in the learning mood. I explained to him that I just cut my hair and that it may be uneven. He told me not to worry that he'd get me together and make sure that once he was finished, I'd be pleased. He asked if there was anything specific that I had in mind.

"I'm sure the only thing you can do is a pixie cut, the only thing I ask is no chemicals. Well, I'm not opposed to color, but no relaxer please."

He spun me around in the chair and took a good look at me. "I'm thinking a wine color and I can curl your hair up real nice. You have enough hang time for me to get it straight without a relaxer."

I laughed and told him that was fine. I checked my phone, ignoring the multiple unread messages that I had and sent Clayton a text to tell him thank you. He was special. I don't know why he had such an interest in me, but I liked it. I felt appreciated, I felt loved, and I felt warm. I was a wreck, but he saw me as a masterpiece. I wasn't just a piece of ass to him. We may not have gone out a handful of times, but the times that we did, he was always thoughtful and took care of me. I was being treated like a queen for once in my life. But I couldn't help but think that maybe this was too good to be true. I hated being this way, but I'd rather be realistic than hold expectations and be disappointed. I still didn't know too much about him. I mean I was really my damsel in distress when I needed sex or needed to feel loved. I was growing comfortable with him sexually. I was forming a liking for him overall, but I needed more. Hopefully we'd grow and become something beautiful. I just felt like he was hiding something though. I had no proof, so I had no choice but to brush it off.

"You're all finished America's next top model!" James turned me in the chair so that I was facing the handheld mirror he had in his hand. I wanted to burst into tears. I was gorgeous! For the first time in the last month, I felt beautiful. I know Clayton would practically bow at my feet when he saw me. I resembled Janelle Monáe, which was my girl crush. I was satisfied, and more importantly I was happy. I thanked James and made my way to the limousine which was sitting right in the front of the salon. As I walked out, all the people in the shop told me how beautiful I looked, and I exchanged their compliments with my gratitude. As I was leaving, I had to do a double take at the young man sitting in one of the barber's chairs. Jonathan. He looked me in the eyes as I continued to leave the barber shop. I didn't think it was appropriate to speak, being that he just left me in the hotel room without the common courtesy of leaving contact information. What we shared was real but obviously not real enough. I was hurt by that, but I also had multiple men in my life that would make up for it. But not being in control of that situation after opening up to him really irritated me. Oh well, I'd have to let it go.

I got in the limo and let the driver close the door after me. He told me we had one more stop before going back to my house. I sat back and enjoyed the ride, trying not to let the curiosity of Jonathan crowd my mind. Tonight, was my night. Clayton and I would have a great time. I felt it in my bones. I couldn't let a stranger fuck this up.

CHAPTER TWENTY-FIVE

We arrived at the Blue Magic Tattoo Lounge in Price hill. There was only one makeup artist that was employed there, so I assumed that's who Clayton made my appointment with. The limo driver opened my door and I practically fell out of my seat. I was excited, and I definitely couldn't hide it no matter how hard I tried.

Zhan'e welcomed me into the shop and into her chair. I had never been here, but I had seen her out quite often. She was cool and seemed very professional.

"Your man set an appointment up for you for tonight. Are you excited?" She asked.

I smiled at her genuinely. "Isn't it obvious?"

She began to cleanse my face. "I've seen you out before. Noel, right?"

I nodded.

"Well I'm Zhan'e, it's a pleasure to meet you. I wish my man would pamper me like this." She began to go on about how she's never really been treated to anything special and how she thought that only tricks got the proper treatment and it wasn't fair. Shit, I agree honestly. This was the first time that I had ever been treated to anything like this and it felt good. I mean, yes, I got a car. But I was being dogged out. This is the first time no bullshit came with it and I was enjoying it.

"I know you don't know what your outfit looks like yet so is it OK if I freestyle? I saw it before-hand so if you trust me, I'll do what I feel is going to compliment it."

I told her that was fine. I just wasn't big on colored lips. She asked if a red lip was too much.

"Wine red is my preference if you absolutely have to. But if not, then nude would be great."

"I was thinking a wine red. I could always put it on and if you don't really like it then I can take it off."

I agreed to that and let her do what she did best. I saw her work and I had no worries at all. There was an established trust between us and I had never even sat in her chair. I sat back and let her paint my face. When I was done, she turned me in the chair and let me look at my face. I wanted to break down in tears once again. I was beautiful. She gave me a cut crease with gold glitter and nude colors, highlight and contour, and a dark wine lip. I loved it! It was just enough makeup, but not too much.

"I look so good. Omg thank you so much!"

Zhan'e smiled. "You look so beautiful, it was seriously my pleasure being able to beat your face!" She was warm and inviting. I liked her, she could possibly be a good new-found friend or an associate. I asked her for her contact information and when she put it in my phone, I bid her farewell. Life was picking up for me. I felt good inside and I wanted to feel like this forever.

—

I remember when I was in high school, the guys never really paid me any attention. I was always attractive, but I wasn't as curious or sexually advanced as everyone else in my class. I was a virgin until I was 17. Most of the girls in my class had lost their virginity by 15. I lost my virginity to a guy I didn't even genuinely like. He was just attractive, and we had been hanging out for quite some time. He and I discussed our desires and ended up becoming intimate. A month later I met Dale, and the rest was history. The guy I gave my most prized possession? Well, I haven't seen him since. He was heartbroken about me and Dale and the month after we made it official, he moved to California with his mom. He didn't bother hitting me up or trying to remain friends. Times like these I wish I kept in touch. Maybe things have changed since we were teenagers. Maybe he was someone worth keeping. But I fucked that up.

—

The driver opened my door to the limo and assisted me as I got in. He complimented me and told me that I was sure to have an amazing night. I hope so I was tired of bad nights and nights where my eyes were so puffy that I didn't want to be seen. I was tired of the mornings that I wouldn't want to wake up. And I was sick and tired of not being able to control my moods and emotions. There were times I would be numb, times I would be sad and hurt to the point I felt it in my chest, there were times I felt defeated, and there were times (even though they were seldom) that I felt like the most beautiful woman in the world and most of all, I would feel free. But that feeling only lasted for a short period of time. I would kill to feel like that all the time. I was lost, and I wanted to be found, not by just anybody though, by myself. I didn't even know who I was anymore. I live day by day like my life doesn't matter. I know that it really does matter, but right now I just feel like it doesn't. I want to change that, but I don't know how. I took my phone out of my pocket and typed in Paisley's name. I didn't want to do this, but I felt like I needed my best friend. I texted, "I need you right now. Can we do lunch tomorrow?" I faced forward and waited to be taken back to my home.

I wonder what Justin was doing. Where the hell was Tisa? Was Dale laid up with his new girlfriend? He probably was. He probably didn't even tell her about me, he was just saying that to get me to hold the baby. I damn near hated him now. He made me feel so useless and I couldn't stop thinking about it. Never in a million years would I have thought I'd be the one going through this shit, especially with him. He was my first love. I've never loved anyone like him. I felt so betrayed. He made me wonder if it was ever real. Was this love or was it comfort? My eyes began to flood. Nope! I look too good to be crying over a manipulating ass nigga. I expanded my lids and let the air dry up my tears. It seems like every time I sit and get the time to think, I'm always in questioning. I couldn't help but wonder why Perez was really in town. Or why I haven't heard from Tisa. Shit, I wanted to know what Justin was about. I know Tisa told me to stay away from him, but it made me want to get to know who he really was and decide if I wanted to fuck with him on my own. I still wanted to know the real reason why Clayton didn't have his car that day. I know he was lying, but I wouldn't ruin our night. I can tell he put a lot of effort into this, a lot of time and most importantly, a lot of money. I'll respect him and talk to him about that later. I just couldn't shake the feeling that something was up. I don't know how to describe it, but I had a bad feeling about everything. If I could afford to move away and start 100 percent over then I would. But now wasn't the time. I'm not sure if it was the people that I was around or if it was just me that needed change. But I didn't really want to stick around and find out. Unfortunately for me, I was broke, and couldn't afford to just pick up and move my life right now. So, Cincinnati had to do for a little while longer.

CHAPTER TWENTY-SIX

We pulled up to my house where Clayton was waiting at the door with flowers. I felt like a bride on her wedding day. Yesterday I hated my hair and my life, but today, I felt like things were looking up. It's crazy how when a man shows you that you are important and that he thinks you are beautiful, you really start to believe it. I'm upset that I couldn't get to this point on my own, but I'm going to appreciate this feeling, no matter who caused it.

He had a polybag hanging off a hanger in his hand, whatever was in it was glistening. And that was good because I loved sparkly things. I was nervous still. Not to sound like a brat, but if I didn't like the dress then I was not going to wear it. I didn't want to hurt his feelings and everything that he has done for me was so perfect thus far. I'm a real simple girl, picky as hell, but simple. I didn't like outrageous attire. The limo driver opened the door and helped me out if the back seat, waiting and watching me until I reached Clayton. I turned and waved to him before I hugged my potential man.

"Thank you so much for everything! I really feel like a queen today. I appreciate you so much." I kissed him on the cheek. He instantly started blushing. "Aww look at you blushing." I began to blush myself and opened the door for him to come inside. He put the dress on the table and sat down on the couch. He was quiet. He seemed eager, nervous maybe, so I broke the ice. I stripped out of my clothes and danced around the first floor of my condo naked. His eyes were set on me while he talked.

"I'm only here to drop off your dress, you're distracting me," he said between smirks. I danced closer to him, feeling completely free. The condo was silent but in my head Janet Jackson's, "Would You Mind" was blasting. Every word of the song was all truth. I wanted to touch him, kiss him, suck him, watch him, and feel him deep inside me. I sang it to him softly, sitting on his lap. He had grey sweat pants on and his dick was rock hard and bulging through. I lightly rubbed my pointer finger on it while it stood up, getting harder and harder.

"You're such a tease," he said looking me in my eyes. "I want you to be my girlfriend."

The statement threw me off, but I kept going. I told him to be quiet and that we would talk about that tonight if everything goes well. He began to kiss me intensely, then I remembered I had on makeup. I pushed him off me and he looked confused.

"My makeup," I said laughing.

"Oh shit, I forgot. It still looks good. I'm sorry babe."

I pushed him on the couch, got up, and started playing with my kitty. I knew she was wet, but sometimes I had to stir the pot and make a mess to make it easier for him to slide in. I sat down on him, ass facing his body. I arched my back as I moaned and took a deep breath.

"We're about to make this quick," he said as he started to stroke deeply. I couldn't control myself. I got louder and louder. I tried to ride while he was stroking, but my knees grew weak and I almost collapsed so I stopped and let him do his thing. He grabbed my neck and went harder, faster, and deeper. I was in so much pleasure, I couldn't even speak. We got off almost at the same time. I tipped over off him right before he came and laid on the couch, lifelessly staring at him as he stared back at me. We were both in a daze until a horn started to beep.

"Let me go, he's waiting for me in the limo. He's supposed to drop me off to get the car."

I looked at him, confused. "What car? I thought we were riding in the limo tonight."

He shook head. "I have something special, just for you. Now, I must go. Get dressed please, and hurry. I'll be back in about 45 minutes." He kissed my forehead.

I sat there and watched him close my door and stared into space for about 10 minutes. Then I rose and walked up the steps, forgetting that the dress was on the table. I took a quick hoe bath and put some shimmering lotion on my collar bone.

Looking in the mirror, I smiled. I haven't done that in a very long time. My heart was warm, and I felt free again. I twirled around naked down the stairs like I was in a musical. I felt great. I wanted to feel like this for the rest of my life. I knew that this feeling wouldn't last though. What's happiness if you have no bad days? If you were always happy you'd soon search for something more. Although I hated my bad days, I was grateful that I had them because my happy days were amplified.

I opened the polybag and my mouth dropped. The dress that he had made for me was *hideous*! I just stood in awe and disappointment. It was a fitted plain white dress with a slit in it, but the bottom had ruffles and the part that was sparkling was under the boob. There was no way I was wearing that. I had to call him and tell him I wasn't going. I dropped the dress and went to find my phone. I didn't want him wasting any more money on a car if I was no longer going. There was no way I was going to be this beautiful in a grandma like ruffled dress. I couldn't find my phone and time was surely ticking. He would be here any minute and I didn't have the balls to tell him to his face. I was practically running down the stairs when I heard the doorbell ring. I stopped and took a deep breath, then yelled for him to come in. To my surprise he opened the door with another polybag in his hand. He was dressed in a navy blue fitted suit with gold accents. I'm not a shoe connoisseur, especially when it came to men's shoes, but I'm sure he had some real gator dress shoes on. He looked amazing. He saw the look on my face and laughed.

"A cruel joke, but it's funny. When were you going to tell me that you didn't like the dress?"

I put my hand on my forehead. "I was searching for my phone getting ready to call you and tell you do not come but I can't find… a joke!? That's not funny Clayton." I walked up to him and snatched the bag out of his hand. "This is mine, right?' I asked before opening.

He nodded and stood in silence watching me open the bag to my real dress. The dress was huge. It didn't look that big in the bag, but I guess the way it was folded gave the impression it was fitted. It was a ball gown, and it was beautiful. Off white and it sparkled in gold to compliment his accents. The top was like a corset, tight and made around my breasts, that's where it sparkled the most. The bottom laid out gracefully with small sparkles throughout.

"Thank you, baby." I smiled. "Help me put it on."

He smiled and bowed. "That must mean that you like it."

I nodded. "I love it!"

The dress had a tie up back, so I needed him to tie it for me. Once he finished, he put a choker around my neck and stepped away, extending his hand.

"Here's your phone," he said handing it to me.

"You took my phone!?" I punched him.

He laughed. "I had to, I didn't want you to call me and ruin the surprise. I didn't go through it or anything. I just kept it in my back pocket. Sorry love."

I rolled my eyes. "I'm ready."

He grabbed my hand and walked me to the couch to sit. "You can't go anywhere without your shoes." He went and grabbed the bag that had the dress in it and reached in the bottom, pulling out a Christian Louboutin box. Then he took the heels out. They were covered with crystals and super high with a platform, just like I liked them. Thank God! This dress was heavy and long so when I put the shoes on, it won't drag on the ground.

"These are cuteeeeee! How much did you spend on all of this?"

"Your mom never taught you not to ask how much something was if you weren't paying for it?"

I rolled my eyes. "OK smart ass, I wanted to give you some of it back. You don't have to do all of this. I appreciate it, I do, but you don't have to spend all of this on me."

"I don't have to, but I want to. And if you're my girl, I'm going to continue to treat you like it. Now, will you be my girlfriend?" He had just finished strapping my shoes and looked me in my eyes.

"You think just because you spend some money I have to be your girl?" I asked. "I just got out of a relationship, Clayton. I like you, but I'm just not ready. I enjoy your time, your energy, and your presence, but I am not complete in myself anymore. I don't want to bring you down while I'm finding myself again."

He shook his head in disappointment. "I understand, but I do want you to know that I'm here to help and build you up.

I'm not going to press you. I'll be patient. But you won't bring me down if I'm lifting you up. We can talk about that later though. Let's go."

I was silent. The way he put things made me feel like I was just making excuses, but I wasn't. I really didn't feel like myself anymore. Plus, I barely knew him enough to jump in a relationship. For all I know, he could be a woman beater, a murderer, or a serial killer just praying on me. They don't always act on the first opportunity they get. I don't think he's that way, but you never know. He could be a manipulator or a whore and I just don't know. Nah, I'm good. I want to get to know him more.

He walked me outside, it was dark now, so I could barely see. I forgot that he said he was going to pick up a car, I was thinking we were getting back into the limo. He opened the door to a two-door blue Rolls-Royce Wraith.

"What the fuck!" I screamed. It glistened in the night sky and I knew this cost him a pretty penny. "Hold up, hold up! Now, how are you an assistant and you can afford to rent a Wraith? Something isn't adding up G."

He told me to shut up and get in. Although he was being playful, I didn't like the fact that there was some weird shit going on go. There was no way he can afford all this on an assistant's salary. I'd figure out what was going on soon enough. He lit a blunt and passed it to me to smoke.

"Relax," he said as he inhaled, "let's just have a good time."

CHAPTER TWENTY-SEVEN

I was pretty high, I'm not going to lie. I'm not sure if it was because it's been a minute since I smoked, or if the weed Clayton bought was a specific strain. Either way I felt good. I washed my kitty after our quickie but the higher I got, the more wet I became. He got me so excited with his clear ass brown skin, his beautiful smile, his effortless charm, and the way he was always calm, even when being expressive. Even the way his breathing made an involuntary gentle hiss. Everything he did made me hot. I did want to be his girlfriend, but I wasn't done living my life. I wasn't finished having fun. I didn't have fun while growing up, because I was committed. I was in my prime. And I didn't have the heart to do him wrong. He was so sweet, so kind and genuine, so handsome, and I'm sure any other woman would have loved to have him. He made me feel like the only girl in the world. I loved that about him. He took care of me. I know it sounds sick, but he did it the way I know my father should have but he didn't. Not in the sense of being family, but in the sense of feeling loved and wanted. Feeling like I held importance. I felt secure when I was around him. I didn't feel the same when I was with Dale, or even when I was with Justin. Justin was just more refreshing, something new. I knew the dangers of being with him and it gave me an adrenaline rush. But like all adrenaline rushes, that soon slowed down.

The ride was quiet. When I get high I became goofy and talkative but with my hormones rising higher and higher, it made me sit back and observe. I didn't want to seem like a freak, we just had sex before we left. I needed to chill.

"I still don't know where we are going," I said over the slow RnB music.

"Your ass is so hard headed. Why can't it be a surprise?"

"I've had enough surprises for the day. I almost had a heart attack." We both laughed.

"We are almost there. Can you behave for this one last surprise?"

I crossed my arms and began to pout like a spoiled brat. "Fine," I said and smiled. "But how much longer until we get there? I feel like we've been in the car for an hour."

"We have 30 more minutes." He turned to me. "Is that alright with you?"

I sarcastically shrugged. "I guess."

He smiled at me and looked straight toward the road. He leaned back in his seat like all the hood niggas I know did.

"How in the hell can you see leaned back like that? I've always wondered." I sat up straight in the passenger seat. "I have to sit all the way up and I can still barely see."

He laughed. "Yeah I've seen you drive, trust me I know." We both laughed.

"Asshole," I mumbled.

"You must be high."

"How you figure?"

"You're talking a lot."

"So, in other words, shut the fuck up?" I asked, laughing.

He didn't laugh. "No. I like when you talk. I like when you communicate with me. Unlike a lot of people, you actually have something to say."

I sat quietly, soaking up everything he said. Is he just ass kissing, or does he really feel like this? I hope he was serious because I was really starting to feel a way about him. I heard about people saying that right after a bad breakup, the love of your life comes along. Maybe that's what this was. I could see myself with Clayton for the rest of my life. Then again, I imagine the rest of my life with any man I deal with. Deep inside I wished it was him that I ended up with. I'm sure I'd want for nothing if we ended up together. As soon as I started to gaze out the window, Beyoncé's, "Upgrade You" started playing. I got super hype and start singing every word to Clayton as if I was talking directly to him. I even started to dance. He just laughed and looked at me like he was proud. Like I was his wife singing our wedding song to him.

"I forgot you can sing. That's so attractive."

I started to blush. "Thank you!" I kissed him on the cheek... then the neck... then on the side of his chin.

He turned away from the wheel. "One more mama."

I then turned and kissed him right on the lips. He tasted like berries and smoke.

"You taste good." I stared him in the eyes before he looked away and refocused on the road.

"You do too."

I blushed again. This exchange between us felt good. I'm ashamed to say that Dale and myself never had one of these moments. It was straight black and white with us. He was affectionate, but not like Clayton. Dale would never hide us but in public, we kept it G rated. With Clayton, he didn't give a fuck where we were or what we were doing. He cared about none of that, he wanted to show me off and was proud to have me by his side. That felt good. I reflected on the previous feelings I had when I was with him. I was nervous and shy, but now I was comfortable with him and comfortable with the fact that this wasn't some game. I didn't have to win or focus all of my time and effort on winning. I wanted to enjoy myself while

I could with this man who's shown me nothing but sincerity and good character. Who knows what tomorrow would bring, but I wasn't worried about that right now. I was finally living in the moment, stress and worry free, the way I needed to be.

—

"We are finally here," Clayton said, interrupting my thoughts. I looked up and focused my attention on the mansion that we pulled up on. Through the gates, there were more than a handful of cars parked around the mansion, all luxury and worth money that I for sure didn't have. I was sure this was a rich affair. I felt like a true bottom feeder at these types of events. I made money, but not anywhere near this type of money. It was a blessing and showed me that these heights are truly obtainable.

We parked, and Clayton stepped outside the car to open my door and help me out. We were parked on concrete, so I didn't worry about my dress being messed up by mud or my heels being dirty, but I was still nervous about falling or embarrassing myself. I was a klutz and the last thing I wanted to do was be embarrassed. I especially didn't want to embarrass him after he put all of this together for me. After helping me out of the car, he spun me around and pulled me close to him.

"I hope you can dance," he said.

My face instantly turned upside down. I couldn't dance for shit. I had no rhythm, something I got from my mom.

"Aww man, you can't dance?"

I shook my head no.

"Well, it's alright, I can't either. I thought you would be able to lead the way. We can just wing it together then." He grabbed my hand, pulling me toward the entrance of the mansion. I was still high, but the feeling of nervousness took over my body. I felt like this every time I was around a bunch of people that I didn't know.

There was music playing, you could tell that the party had started but there was a rush at the door, so there was a line in front of a security guard in a suit with a list. I'm assuming this was an invite only party. Clayton led me to the front of the line.

"What's the name?"

"Clayton Davis."

"What's your plus one's name?" The guard looked at me then back at him.

"It should have already been on there but, Noel Gray." He nodded his head and stepped to the side, letting us bypass the entire line and the other two guards standing on each side of him. As we entered the home, I admired the marble floors and high ceilings. The entryway led to an open ball room like area. I assumed that's where we were going, but when I began to veer off that way, Clayton grabbed my hand and led me in a different direction.

"I thought that was the ballroom?" I asked, embarrassed.

He shook his head and slightly chuckled. "Nope, you'll see." I was curious at this point. This was a huge estate with a ballroom in the middle of the entryway, and that wasn't where they were hosting their party. I guess there was another area in the house, either that or we were going outside. I didn't want to sound like a brat, but I put on perfume and smell good lotion before I came. If we were going to be outside, I was surely going to leave with a thousand mosquito bites.

"Are we going outside?"

He looked at me and smiled. "No, Noel. Relax. You'll see in just a second."

We walked past the kitchen that had white marble countertops, a nice elegant sparkling chandelier, and a huge dining room table. There was an island in the middle of the room that was shining with marble as well. I had never been in a mansion before, and I honestly was ashamed. I grew up super poor and I had never been in a large house of any sort. Everyone I knew had apartments and if they did have a larger house, their whole family lived there, and everything was cramped. This was motivation.

We passed all types of rooms in route to our destination. The one I paid the most attention to was a sun room where there were yoga mats and white and gold tapestry all along the walls. There was a pyramid type of fixture sitting on the floor. This must have been the zen room. I was so jealous! I wasn't super spiritual and in touch with my natural side, but I was getting there. I researched everything about spirituality and inner peace and was infatuated with it.

We made it upstairs to the grand ballroom. Blue lights covered the ceilings and tables that were covered in white table cloths and complemented with gold accents. The floor was dark carpet, I couldn't make the color out because of the neon blue lights. The dance floor was a white marble, matching the interior decoration of the house. The ballroom was already halfway full. From the looks of it, there could probably be at least one thousand people inside without it being a fire hazard. There was some elevator music playing, probably so that people could socialize before the event started.

"It's beautiful, isn't it?"

I just nodded my head. I was speechless for real.

"I'm going to get us one." He said and looked me in the eyes.

I laughed but his face stayed serious. "I take it you weren't joking?"

He tilted my chin up at him. "Baby girl, stop playing with me. You know I want you to be my woman. And I'm waiting for you. Anything you want, you can have. I guarantee you'll get there on your own because you're smart, focused, and dedicated, but together we can really make this happen."

I just stared at him. Not because I was trying to brush off the fact that this man was serious about me, but because I didn't know what to say. I've never had a man bring me out to any fancy event. I've never had a man really invest his time into me or be as sweet as he was.

"Show me," I finally said after deep thought. If anything, I didn't want to fall for a false prophet. Yeah, Clayton has showed me a lot. He's backed up his word many times but that doesn't mean that he is going to follow through with such a heavy commitment. We haven't known each other that long. I like him, and I finally let my guard down with him a little. I realized that he wasn't playing a game. I stopped taking our relations and making it a competition. I had to get out of the mindset that he just wanted to come out on top. If that was the case, then I'd just take that L. Walking around with that mentality will just make things worse. I could potentially lose a good man. It can honestly go either way, I could miss out or I could waste my time. But you miss 100 percent of the shots that you don't take, so I'll just take my chance.

Everyone was dressed so beautifully. I felt like I was at a celebrity event. Where I'm from, events like this could barely get attendees. Not because they didn't want to come, but because no one had the appropriate attire.

"Who made my dress?" I forgot to ask before.

"My sister did. She lives in Dayton. You probably never heard of her."

"Oh, OK. She did a great job."

"Yeah, she's been designing for years now. She has a shop downtown. I'm going to have her do my costume design when I create my first film."

"I never did get to ask, what exactly in film do you do? Are you interning like me, or did you just need a gig?"

"Not exactly." He motioned for me to sit down at a table.

"I don't really need a gig. It's more like, I need connects and opportunity. Dayton is a small city, and you can only get so far with what I'm doing up there. I am a videographer trying to get more into film. All I did there was shoot music videos and commercials for people. Although it's decent money, it's not enough. I want to further my career to the big screen. Can't do that being small minded with small minded people."

I nodded. "Yeah, I understand. Yes, working with Tisa, you'll get the opportunity and exposure. What kind of movie are you going to create? Do you want to write it? Or are you going to hire someone to do that?" I was curious. We never talked about this, which is backwards as fuck, but it's never too late.

"I want to hire you." He held my hand. I'm sure he felt that I was nervous.

"You've never even seen or read my work," I said with a little attitude. "I could be horrible, with a cute face."

"Nah, you wouldn't work for Tisa if you were trash. This I know."

I laughed. "OK, so what kind of film do you want? Let me get started then."

"So, I know it's going to sound crazy but, I really want to create a special effects film, some super fantasy. But I can't wrap my hands around what I want the story line to be. That's why I want to hire you. I know you are very creative and can come up with something that would be amazing, if you're willing. And of course, we can talk about your pay."

He continued talking, I zoned out thinking about winning a Grammy based off the film that I created for him. I had dreams of being a big film writer. I just hadn't had the opportunity to create yet. I was going to wait until I finished with school to start, but why limit myself.

I interrupted him. "I can do that! Give me a few days to brainstorm and we'll talk."

He nodded and right when he was about to respond, someone came and interrupted our conversation.

"Well, hey beautiful!" Her smile was big, and she looked familiar. I had to look at her twice to realize who she was.

"Hey girl!" I said, getting up to hug her. It was Perez. "I'm starting to think you're following me."

She laughed and winked. "Maybe I am. Anyway, I just wanted to let you know that you look great! And you guys look amazing together! Who's your friend, Noel?"

I had to laugh because she was being nosey and pretty bold if you ask me.

"Perez, this is my boyfriend Clayton."

He looked surprised and shook her hand. "Nice to meet you Perez." He smiled, looking clueless.

"Oh, boyfriend. Well, he definitely complements your beauty. I'll see you guys around. I'm going to get a drink." She twirled away in her flowing navy-blue dress, which did look good on her by the way. I just didn't like the way she did that. I rolled my eyes.

"She might as well have asked for your number." I said sarcastically.

"Jealous?" He smiled.

"No! That was just rude as hell."

"Relax babe. I'm not interested in her. I'm here with you," he reassured me.

"But still, that was just out of line to me," I said rolling my eyes again.

"So, are we just going to disregard the fact that you just claimed me as your boyfriend?" he asked sarcastically.

"Shut up." I tried to keep a straight face, but I burst into laughter. "You're my boyfriend tonight while these vultures are out that's for sure."

"Nah, nah, that's not how this works! If I'm your boyfriend, then I'm your boyfriend from here on out!" He smiled. "You can't just play with my emotions."

I smiled. "OK, whatever you want king."

He had the biggest smile when I told him that. Well I'm in a relationship now I guess. He got up and grabbed my hand.

"I'm going to get us a drink at the bar, I'll be back. You want something light?"

I nodded. He kissed my forehead and I watched him walk away and smiled. This could be the beginning of something good.

CHAPTER TWENTY-EIGHT

The room began to fill up as the night grew old. Everyone was laughing and having fun, smiling, socializing, and enjoying themselves. There were a few other people that sat down at our table. I had small talk with them until Clayton came back with our drinks. I kept forgetting to ask whose party this was. I was too busy enjoying myself that I forgot that he never told me why we were here or who we were celebrating.

When I was with Dale, I didn't do much. I didn't really have a social life. Everything was school and work, and if it wasn't that then it was all about him. When I was with Clayton I had fun, I explored, I tried new things, I did what I liked. He opened me up to a new side of myself. Somewhere over the past three years, I lost myself and gave my life to a man. A man that didn't even come home half of the time. A man that had a child behind my back and lived an entire double life. I was 23, waiting up at night for him to come home, trying to keep up with him, and I still failed. I should be living my life. I hated to admit it, but Clayton changed me. He changed me for the better. Not only has he introduced me to what it feels like to be appreciated, he's shown me that there is way more to life than sitting at home babysitting and playing detective. He gave me that confidence and made me step up and make gradual effort to take charge of my life. I was still depressed from time to time, but you can't recreate yourself without breaking and losing yourself first. There were times I didn't feel like getting out of the bed, times where I couldn't do anything but breathe. There were times I wanted to be held, times that I wanted to feel like I mattered, but I didn't. I wanted to hurry my life and be successful, so I could live lavishly and splurge when I wanted. I was constantly thinking about more and how I could improve. I got so caught up in the mores that I forgot to be grateful for what I already have. It's like I've programed myself to be negative. We all need to strive to be better in every aspect, but to just forget about how far we've come is ungrateful.

—

Maybe I was overthinking, but the fact that I kept running into Perez was a little weird. She lived in Queens and although she told me that she was visiting for an acting audition, I didn't really believe that. Why the hell would she be invited to this event? And now that I am thinking about it, she never mentioned acting. I wasn't paying that much attention to her and Paisley talk the day we stopped at her house, but I could have sworn she said that she was a dancer. I could be wrong though.

Clayton came back to the table with one highball glass of Goose and cranberry, my drink of choice, and a lowball glass filled with dark liquor.

"Let me guess, Henny?"

He nodded. "Henny and lemonade."

I was curious, so I took a sip, and surprisingly it was tasty. I hated dark liquor, and I hated Hennessy even more (Hennessy and D'ussé were the typical "nigga drink."). But that was pretty good.

"Who's party is this anyway?"

"A friend of mine just signed a deal with Universal, so he decided to have a formal gathering. He should be out soon. This is his uncle's house. He's an anesthesiologist and also has his hands in some real estate and a few restaurants in Miami."

I just shook my head. Those are the type of accomplishments that I wanted. I wanted a big estate, a large bank account, and a few businesses. Now days, everyone was in competition and social media didn't make it any better. Social media made people feel like they were behind in life. That was mainly the reason why I didn't post much. I did watch though, because I must keep up the media for my profession.

Clayton's friend was Eric Bates. I heard of him before. When he arrived at the party, everyone clapped and shouted in celebration. We all did a toast and the DJ turned up the music. Clayton took my hand and bowed as I got up out of the chair.

"I have to tell you a secret."

He looked at me with a nervous expression.

"I can't dance." I put my head down in shame.

He laughed and assured me that I was OK. He told me to just follow his lead and to relax. I can't lie, I was nervous as fuck. One wrong move in this dress and I was going to topple over, slip, and fall, embarrassing us both. I took a deep breath and tried to calm myself. I was very shy when it came to anything being done in front of a crowd. He led me to the dance floor and held me close. There was a group of people standing, dancing, and enjoying themselves. The turnout was great and there wasn't a dull person in the room. We gazed into each other's eyes and couldn't help but to smile. I felt like I was falling in love. I was still indecisive as hell. I still wanted to dip and dab with other men. And that was the entire reason that I didn't want to start a relationship with him. He was way too good for me. I was still learning about him. I honestly wasn't ready, but I already agreed to it, so I couldn't take it back. Truth is, I wanted him for myself while I was still at liberty to do what I wanted to do with whoever I wanted to do it with, but I didn't want to share him at all. If I was to see him with another woman or to even hear about him being with someone else, I would feel some type of way. I was being selfish. It was wrong. I knew I wasn't finished with Justin; I was way too curious, and I knew that I wanted to explore my options sexually. But I didn't want him to deal with anyone but me.

The music was slow. At an event like this, I thought there would be classical music playing, but they played slow RnB. The first song we danced to was "If This World Were Mine" by Luther Vandross and Cheryl Lynn. That was my absolute favorite love song! The first time I watched *The Wood* I fell in love with it. I told him that I wanted this to be my wedding song. He agreed that it was a beautiful song and told me that we would talk about it. I smiled. He was everything. He was respectful, genuine, caring, loving, and made me feel like I was a better woman than I was.

As we continued to dance, I drifted away into deep thought. My life was still a mess. I was lost for real. I deadass liked Clayton, but I still wanted to hoe. I liked Justin too. I knew he was probably going to end up bad for me, but I still wanted the thrill. I still thought about Jonathan from time to time, but he clearly wasn't that interested. My living situation was cool but at any moment Dale could pull back on our agreement. I didn't want that to happen and I be ass out. I mean, I guess I wouldn't really be out of a place to stay because I now had a boyfriend, I could stay with him. But I wanted my freedom. If I needed space I wanted to be able to go to my house. Hell, I've never even been to Clayton's house. I had to stop my thought process and address that.

"How am I going to be your girlfriend and I've never even been to your house?" I asked with a little attitude.

"I mean, you never asked. You can come to my house tonight. Mi casa es tu casa," he said, looking me in the eyes.

"I think I'll take you up on that." As soon as I turned my head, I caught eyes with Perez. Her brown face was glistening with gold highlight. I can't lie, she looked good. Paisley must have made her up. She smiled at me and kept eye contact. I ended up turning my head and getting back to the conversation with Clayton. My vagina was wet already but for some reason tonight, Perez turned me on.

"How do you know her?" he asked, startling me.

"Well, I was in New York on business with my old best friend Paisley and that was her friend. We stopped by her house in Queens. I'm just trying to figure out why she's here. I ran into her at Walmart about a week ago and I asked her why she was here. She told me she was an aspiring actress here for an audition. But something just doesn't seem right. You're observant," I said and took his hand leading him in the direction of the bar.

"She looks like she likes you."

I agreed. "I'm starting to think she does."

"Are you into women?"

I shrugged. "Not sure, I've never tried it. I don't mind exploring. I just don't know if I'd like it or not. Why? Do you not like that?"

He put his hand on his chin, scratching his full beard. "Well, I'm not necessarily against it, but I want you all to myself. I don't want to share you with anyone, especially another woman."

I understood. Most men liked that shit but there were some out there that didn't care for it.

"Have you ever had a threesome?"

"Nope." He shrugged.

"Want one?" I asked smiling mischievously. I'm not going to lie I've always wanted to have one just for fun.

"Oh, you with the shits. I mean I don't mind. If you're comfortable with it. You're plotting on her?"

We laughed. And I smiled again. "Let me see if I can get her, I'm sure that won't be hard at all. She was already on your ass." I rolled my eyes.

"You sure this is a good idea?"

"Yeah, I'm confident that you won't keep in contact with her after it happens. As long as we have that understanding, we're good." I wasn't worried about Clayton communicating with Perez afterward if we did go through with this. I trusted him in a sense. And if he did decide to communicate with her, then I'd just leave him. After everything that happened with me and Dale, my tolerance was low. One wrong move, you had to go. If you give a person an inch they will surely take it a mile. But I just don't think he's the type.

"You're the boss, I wouldn't do that anyway. That's crossing the line."

"Well, we're good then. Let me see what I can do." I leaned over the bar counter and asked the bartender for another round of drinks. We waited by the bar until she was finished making them and I gave Clayton his drink.

"Go sit down for a second, babe. I'll be right back."

He went and sat at our table. I made my way across the room to where Perez was standing in line for the shutter booth. I stood behind her, she was last in line.

"Did I tell you that you looked nice tonight? You look stunning. I love your hair!"

She had colored her natural hair blond and it was nothing short of complementing.

"No, but thank you love. I appreciate it." She smiled.

"How was your audition?" I didn't really know how to go about organizing a threesome, so I started winging it.

"It was great! I think I have it. They usually call two to three weeks after the auditions with results if you were picked."

"How long are you here? If you don't mind me asking."

"I leave tomorrow. I wish I could have spent some more time with you."

I wasn't expecting that response. "You can spend some time with us tonight, my boyfriend and I that is. After the party, if you want we can all hang out or grab something to eat. What time are you leaving tomorrow?"

"Early, 10:00 in the morning. But I would love to hang with you guys. They're feeding us here, so I doubt we will need to eat anything else though."

"Oh, I didn't know, well good! Yeah, if you want, you can ride back to my spot with us after."

She shook her head and reached in her purse to grab her phone. "Put your number in my phone, I'll call you."

I put my number in her phone and walked back over to Clayton at the table. I was infatuated with his skin. It was so clear and smooth. Every time I looked at him I got excited.

"Well I invited her over," I said sitting down. "I'm sure she got the hint. But we have to go to my house because I don't want her first time at your place to be my first time too." I picked my drink up and took a sip.

"That's cool, you can come to my place tomorrow. I'll make you lunch. Better yet, do you want to go get a massage? I've never had one, and we are both off tomorrow."

"Yes, that sounds great, honestly. I've never had one either, so this'll be fun." I was excited about getting a massage. I needed one, I was stressed.

We danced until the party was over. I still get butterflies when I'm around him. He made me nervous. It was in a good way though. Perez texted me and made sure I had her number, although we were still in the same room. She said she would get a ride to my house. I texted her my address a little bit before we left. I was drunk. My high was gone but I felt super warm inside. I wanted to light up again when we got to my house. It would be fun. I was soaking wet through my thong. The thought of a threesome made me hot. I wanted it now. Me drinking just intensified my desire. Every time Clayton touched me, I felt a chill all over my body. I was more than ready from all the liquid courage. I had plenty to drink between when I sat back down from giving Perez my number and leaving the party. Now it was time to let loose. Technically she didn't agree to a threesome, but I'm sure she would. I can just tell that she's down. She had a mystery to her that I liked. And even if she didn't, I still was going home with my man, so everything would work out just fine.

CHAPTER TWENTY-NINE

The ride home was long and slow. I fell asleep to the music blasting. Clayton was a little tipsy, but he never got drunk, especially while driving. Perez texted me and said she had left from the party early, she was going to make a stop and then head over to my place. Clayton had to wake me up when we got home. There was a surprise waiting on us. Dale's Suburban was sitting in the driveway. As soon as I saw it, I rolled my eyes. What the hell was he doing there? I'm sure he's just going to cause more trouble.

"Huuuuuuuh! What the fuck does he want?" I mumbled under my breath.

"Do you want me to stay in the car?"

"No, come in with me. You're my boyfriend. We made agreements for me to keep the condo. I'm definitely getting my locks changed tomorrow." I got out of the car, almost stumbling over my long ball gown. I took my shoes off when I first got in the car, I reached back in the passenger seat and grabbed them. Clayton stood at the front of the car and waited for me. He usually opened my door for me, but I got out so fast I didn't give him a chance to. I stormed to the door and realized that it was open. Walking in with Clayton on my trail, my mouth dropped and I instantly became irate. There were candles lit everywhere with balloons and rose petals leading up the steps. Dale was nowhere to be found. I looked back at Clayton, he was just as confused as I was. I didn't say a word. I went up the steps into my bedroom, and there was Dale setting up my bedroom for some type of romantic night.

"What the fuck are you doing? What are you doing here?" I yelled, startling him.

"A 'thank you' would be nice," he said turning toward me.

I just looked at him, I was pissed. My new boyfriend was probably thinking I still had something going on with my ex, and that was so far from the truth.

"Get out!" My blood was beginning to boil at this point.

He had a confused look in his eyes. "Did I miss something?"

"What the fuck do you mean? Get out! You are not welcome here! Give me your key. Stay away from me. I don't want to see you. I don't want you to dress up the house, I want you out of my life for good." I couldn't control myself. I don't understand why he thought it would be acceptable to do this. But the thought of him even trying to get on my good side made me more and more livid. I was embarrassed and now I had to explain this to my boyfriend.

"I was just trying to…"

I had to cut him off because if I let him talk, this would be even more of a situation then it already was.

"I don't care what… You know what? Can you please just leave and go home to your family? Please. And don't come back. I don't want to rekindle anything, I don't want anything to do with you. We are done Dale. Finished. There is nothing left to talk about. Am I clear?"

He just looked at me and nodded. His lips spread, and it looked as though he was going to cry. That wasn't my issue.

"OK, keep the decorations." He grabbed his belongings and stormed out of what was now my bedroom. I sat on the bed and shook my head. I was shaking, that's how mad I was. Clayton came up the steps and sat down next to me.

"Are you OK?" He rubbed the side of my face.

"Yeah, I'm cool. I just don't understand why he would think that any of this was OK. I haven't talked to him since we decided that he would no longer be staying here, and I can keep the condo. He popped up with his daughter that he had behind my back and started trying to force me to hold her and all type of bull shit." I didn't tell him about the other time I saw him, when we had sex and I kicked him out afterward. But Clayton didn't need to know that. So, I continued with the lie.

"I came up here and he said I should be thanking him. As if I asked for him to come here and try and make amends. I've been just fine without him. Now I got you looking at me like

I'm still dealing with him and shit when I don't. I swear, I don't even talk to him." Tears began to form in my eyes. These weren't sad tears, I was tearing up because I was pissed and wanted to fight. I got so worked up and couldn't do anything about it. Such a beautiful night Clayton had planned, and it was all ruined because of my ex- boyfriend.

"How can I make things better?" He kissed me on the cheek. He was so selfless. That's what I loved about him. Right when I was about to answer him, the doorbell rang. It was Perez.

"Can you get that babe?" I asked him as I began taking off my dress.

He smiled and got up to get the door. I honestly wasn't even in the mood anymore. But I had already invited her. I wasn't even thinking, I took off my dress and walked down to the living room in my bra and thong. When I greeted her, her eyes lit up, making me realize that I was in fact half naked. I quickly apologized, I didn't want to offend her. She told me it was OK. I think she liked the sight of my half naked body. We all sat down on the couch and turned on the TV. Clayton rolled up and we all had small talk. Perez looked comfortable. I didn't know how to pitch the idea that we wanted to include her in a threesome. And I'm sure Clayton wasn't going to say anything. I didn't want to press it, so I didn't say anything, I just felt out the vibes and if everything went in that direction, I'd speak up.

We sat for about an hour and a half talking, laughing, and smoking. We lost track of time. She said she had to leave in the morning, so I told her she could stay the night. She agreed. I grew tired, so I told her that I was going to bed, and she could sleep in the guest bedroom. She asked if she could use the shower and I told her that was fine. Excusing myself to the second floor of the condo, I grabbed two towels and washcloths, one for her and me. I was sweaty from all the dancing and partying I did that night. I placed her towel and washcloth on the counter in the guest bathroom and checked the room to make sure that there was nothing she would need. I hollered down the steps and told her that everything was ready for her. Clayton had made his way upstairs and began to undress in the bedroom and get ready for bed. Perez didn't advance so I left it alone. I told him that I was going to shower before getting in bed. I was still high, so I took off my bra and thong slowly. I looked in the mirror, my makeup was still intact from earlier that day. I still looked good. I didn't want to wash the makeup off. I felt so beautiful. But all good things come to an end.

Turning the shower on, I made sure that the water was hot. I loved my showers steamy. I admired my body before stepping in. Letting the water run over me, I took a deep breath. Whenever I was high, everything intensified. Every feeling was multiplied times 10, and every experience was heightened. I thought I heard a knock at the door, but I ignored it because I thought I was tripping. If it was Clayton, he would have just walked in. A second knock came, and the door opened slightly.

"Can I come in?" It was Perez.

"Yeah, you can come in. I'm in the shower. What's up?" I think I already know what she wanted.

"Would it be alright if I took a shower with you?"

I chuckled to myself. I wasn't sure at first if she had really got the hint I was throwing at her, but now I was certain. I knew she was into me. I had a strong feeling. I'm glad that she came around.

"Yes, you can, I didn't want to make you uncomfortable."

"I think we both knew that I was interested. Have you ever been with a woman before?"

"No, but I've watched enough porn. I'm sure I'll pick up quickly." I moved over in the shower so she could get in.

She smiled and pushed me against the shower door, rubbing my nipples lightly, then sliding down between my legs, letting the water run down her body and her hair. The straight blunt cut bob that she had quickly turned into a curly natural fro. She spread my legs and placed her hands on the door, letting the steam fill me up inside.

"Relax," she whispered as she licked on my thighs and kissed my clit.

I felt chills run through my body as she continued to kiss all over my flower. I tried not to be too loud. I didn't stop and let Clayton know all of this was happening. I wasn't being secretive or sneaky, but I didn't want to be loud as hell and have him wondering what was going on. He wasn't the thirsty type, he wouldn't burst in the door because he heard moaning going on. I'm sure if he heard us, he would know what was going on.

She didn't stop, and I didn't want her to, it felt so good. I rubbed my hands through her hair and called out in pleasure. She stuck her finger in my kitty and went in and out slowly. I came within minutes. My body tensed, and I struggled to breathe. I was overwhelmed. I didn't know that this would feel this good. I've had plenty of head from men before, and it never felt like this. I'm not sure if it was just because I was high, or if it was because I was more excited in general because it was a woman doing this. Either way, I felt amazing. I felt like I was in the clouds. I came about three times. Each time my body tensed up, she started licking faster. I took a deep breath, I was slightly exhausted. She came up for air and started to kiss all over me. I kissed her back and we locked lips kissing more intensely. I asked her if she would mind if Clayton joined. She smiled. We washed each other's bodies. Seeing the bubbles all over her turned me on all over again. We rinsed each other then dried off. We took turns oiling each other up, taking advantage of the opportunity to touch some more. I then grabbed her hand and led her to the bedroom where Clayton was stretched out on the bed. He was fixing another joint, his eyes glossy and red when he looked up at us, both naked and coated with oil, giggling our way closer to him. He had a quiet nature, so he didn't say much but he looked to me as if he was asking for permission. I released Perez's hand and made my way to the bed. My back arched, ass in the air, and my legs extended. I lifted the covers from over him, revealing his bare legs and penis. It was lying on his leg, solid and pulsating. I've seen this man naked plenty of times, but this time I was infatuated. I kissed the tip of his dick and slowly sucked on it. I began to lick the bell head, getting it wet then I stopped. Perez was at the edge of the bed watching. I got up and laid her on her back next to Clayton and opened her legs. She was hairless and clean, her skin was smooth and her flower petals tight and intact. I lifted her legs and rubbed my hands all the way down to her calves, pushing them back next to her head. Her breasts were small, and nipples resembled gum drops. Small simple rose gold nipple rings pierced through her nipples and spilled out into her areola. I drew my attention back to her pretty pussy. I had never done this before, but I felt like I knew what I was doing. I made sure my mouth was wet like I was about to give a man head and took the tip of my tongue and twirled it around her clit slowly. She started to moan uncontrollably. I took my entire tongue and made my way from the inside of her lips back up to the clitoris. I was so focused that I didn't even notice Clayton getting up. He placed his hands on my ass cheeks and began to lick my clit down to my ass hole. I had to stop and break from eating Perez. She took her middle finger and played with her clit as I leaned back down and finished what I started. I was dripping wet. Clayton took his dick and slid himself inside me. He started off slow and deep and began to speed up.

"Shit!" I screamed while trying to continue to lick Perez's cat. My pussy dripped all over his dick, there was cream everywhere. This time more than usual. He stuck his thumb in my butt and repositioned my ass in the air, forcing himself deeper inside me. I wasn't great at multitasking, I got sidetracked from Perez to focus on Clayton's penetration. Perez got up and moved toward Clayton on the bed. He flipped me over on my back and Perez jumped on top of me rubbing her clit against mine, tooting her ass in the air. Clayton stopped in the middle of his tracks and looked at me. I nodded my head and told him it was OK. He entered Perez and she began to go wild. She was a little smaller than me and watching her be penetrated by my man turned me on even more.

I sucked on her breasts as she bounced in the rhythm of his stroke. He let her throw it back on him. She kissed all over my body and gripped my breasts, and Clayton let out small whimpers. He pulled out of her and she got off me. I got up and began to kiss Clayton passionately, turning him around and laying him on his back. I got on top of him and began to ride him, letting my ass clap on top of his dick. Perez rode his face and looked back at me moaning. I started riding harder and more passionately. My mind traveled to many dimensions. I saw all sorts of colors, from blue to magenta to green and purple. Paint splatters ran across my eyes with the silhouette of Perez's body in the background. I screamed involuntarily and began to shake uncontrollably. I looked down, snapping out of my love spell, and saw that there was cream everywhere. I continued to ride him until I was out of breath and collapsed on the side of him. Perez hopped off his face and laid on the bed. And Clayton laid still, breathing heavily. From the looks of things, we all came and were satisfied. I passed out laying my head on his chest, with her body next to mine. There we lay, the night watching us sleep.

CHAPTER THIRTY

I woke up screaming. I was startled, and Clayton was too. I hushed him back to sleep. I had a nightmare. This was the first time I stayed the night at his house, and I had a horrible nightmare. I was probably overthinking it, but I felt like this was a sign. I don't know what it was, but something just wasn't right.

Yesterday was great! We went and got massages, went to Pappadeaux and had my favorite meal, went to the park and had ice cream, then had a movie night. I wouldn't imagine that

I would have nightmares tonight. I couldn't go back to sleep. I was wide awake, but I didn't want to wake my boyfriend.

In my dream, I was in a terrible car accident and ended up in a comma for a while. I felt like it was real. I lost sight of the road and flipped over in a ditch after running into another car. While in this comma, I was dressed in a long flowy dress and a lot of heavy jewelry. My hair was long and curly again. I kept seeing demons and weird looking gargoyles trying to lead me somewhere. My guess is death. They were all pretty and gold with glitter shimmering all over their bodies. They danced with me, slowly pulling me away, but I fought it and danced the opposite direction. Then right before I woke up, a portal opened, and they ran and jumped inside uncovering a red and sweaty beast. This beast was quiet and still at first, just looking directly in my eyes. Then it touched my face, it didn't say anything. Then I suddenly heard a soft voice that told me that I had to choose. And before I chose, it grabbed me by the neck and chose for me. That's when I woke up. I was scared, I didn't understand. Everything in my life was going fine right now other than the fact that my best friend and I weren't speaking. We were supposed to meet to talk again but she never returned my call. That may have been for the best. I wanted to talk to someone about my dream, but I couldn't. They'd only tell me that it was only a nightmare and that I shouldn't worry about it. I remembered what my grandmother told me; if I ate heavy before I went to bed then I would have a higher chance of having a nightmare. I didn't eat anything heavy last night. I ate hours before bed and that was ice cream. I was hungry. I laid next to Clayton absorbing his body heat, getting comfortable in bed. He was out cold, so I spooned him. I felt like a mother holding her baby. He was my baby. He made the most tremendous impact on my life. I didn't want to let him go. I kissed his bare back and closed my eyes, eventually drifting back to sleep.

—

"Noel, I'm going to the store then I have to go in and meet with Tisa. Did you want to come?" I was still tired from the night before. "No, I think I'll pass," I did not want to go into work when I didn't have to.

"OK, are you staying here?" He handed me a key.

"For a while, then I have to go. I have to go back to New York to handle some business."

He stopped in his tracks and looked at me in silence. "If I didn't know any better, I'd think you had a secret lover out there."

I rolled my eyes at him and sat up. "Nope, I just like making money. You're all I need." I smiled.

"Yeah alright," he said as he grabbed his keys, making his way toward me. He kissed my forehead and began to walk away. I pulled him back and drew his lips into mine, kissing him softly. "Call me when you get to your destination," he said and left the bedroom.

Clayton wasn't stupid. He knew what was going on. I couldn't tell him. I had to break it off with Justin. Clayton was such a good guy and I didn't want to make things between us go sour. I liked Justin, but he was a huge risk. A risk to my relationship and apparently a risk to my life. I'd tell him when I saw him that I had to leave him alone. Truthfully, I didn't want to, I still wanted deal with him. He made me feel good.

When Clayton left, I called Justin and told him that I got the email confirmation for the flight in four hours. He told me he'd have his driver come get me from the airport and bring me to one of his properties because he'd be in the field when I arrived. I agreed and hung up the phone. I was eager. I wanted to make myself believe that I wasn't. I had to get in the mindset to let him go. I had a good man and I didn't want to mess it up. But Justin just felt so good. Again, he was a temporary high, but I wanted to indulge in him repeatedly. But I had to cut it off. I'd be kicking myself about it later if I didn't.

I showered, got dressed, cleaned up the house a little, and left so I could go home and pack a small bag. I was off until Tuesday, I got a lot of my work done so that I wouldn't have to be in the office. Usually, I wanted to come in anyway, but I wasn't really feeling Tisa right now. It was something that she was hiding from me and I knew it. I just had no proof. I didn't want to keep pressing her about it because then she would know that I'm still dealing with Justin. Now that Clayton and I were official, that just wasn't smart. I didn't want to ruin my relationship over a thug. I was so fond of him, I wasn't sure if she would tell him about it or not. I needed to end things fast before he mentions that I was in New York again and she puts two and two together and accidentally tells him. I was convincing myself that I could do it and that I had to cut all ties. I knew it would be hard because of the way I felt when I was around him and because of how mysterious he was. Even though I knew some of his background and that he wasn't involved in good things, that didn't mean that he was a bad person. I wanted to get to know the real him. Plus, I'm not going to lie, I liked the fact that he has money.

—

I made my way to the airport. I flew Delta first class. It was cool. I appreciated the little things, but I was OK with flying economy. The perks of first class weren't really needed for this trip. I was going and leaving, I didn't need any extra bags. I wasn't hungry, and I was still cold. I saw the air come out of the vents, it looked like steam. I had on a hoodie and I was still freezing. The cold always irritated me.

I let everyone pass me up while exiting my flight. I was in no rush to see Justin and cut ties. I was in no rush to return home. I yearned for time away. I couldn't stop thinking about that nightmare I had.

His driver picked me up in a chrome black Hummer. I can already tell this was going to be a bad day. I hated Hummers. The thought of them made me cringe. The fact that I had to ride in one made me sick. I felt like this was a sign. I got in anyway and rode to my destination. The driver didn't speak, he just told me when we arrived. The skies were grey and crying for attention. The sorrow written in the sky made me weak. I felt it in my bones. I had a sudden feeling of exhaustion and remorse. He told me that the door would be open, and Justin would arrive shortly. The driver offered to let me wait in the car, I declined. I wanted to clear my head and I couldn't do that with him clouding my energy. I stepped out of the car and grabbed my bag. I waved to the driver and walked in the house. It was fully furnished with expensive décor. There were marble floors like the ones that I saw at the estate Clayton took me too, except they were black with white marble and not the other way around. The countertops were granite and black matching the floors and the furniture was snow white. The house looked great! I walked around observing and imagining that this was my place. I loved it. I gave myself a tour, ignoring the basement door. I didn't go in basements, especially alone in unfamiliar places. They creeped me out. I sat in the living room next to the kitchen with a clear view of the front door so that when Justin walked in, I'd see him face to face. Being in a house that I knew nothing of just gave me the jitters. I sat and waited for a while before I called Justin, he didn't answer but sent me a text immediately after saying that he was held up with his last client and would be there soon. I turned the TV on, kicked my feet up, and made myself at home. The lights were off, it was midday but of course there were dark skies outside. I was tired and began to drift off to sleep.

—

I suddenly woke up to a loud *boom*. I jolted up and looked around the room. I didn't see anything, but I didn't want to move either. I just sat still trying to listen past the TV. I didn't want to turn the volume down and draw attention to myself if there was someone in the house. I text Justin and told him about what I just heard. I was afraid that someone was in the house with me. I got up and tiptoed around. I moved slowly, trying not to make a sound. I made it all the way past the kitchen and then I felt a whiff of air brush past me. I turned around instantly and felt someone grab me and force their hand around my neck, the hand was strong and muscular. I tried to break free and scream but I was losing so much oxygen I couldn't make a sound. The man was masked, and he was saying something. I was too overwhelmed to hear or even try to make it out. He struggled to keep a hold on me. I was small, but I was strong. I almost broke free. Then the door burst open and Justin walked in with a gun in his hand pointed at the masked man. I was out of breath when the man threw me on the ground and pointed a gun at me. He walked toward me and shrugged his shoulders. Justin stood still with the gun still pointed at the masked man. The house was silent.

"You have 10 seconds to make a decision," the masked man said as he moved closer to me, gun still pointed at my head. The gun wasn't right next to my head, he was about a foot away which told me that he didn't really have any intention on shooting me for real. He wanted Justin. The man began to countdown. I looked up at Justin straight faced. I wasn't afraid to die. It was the act of surprise that had me on my toes. If I knew that I was going to die and how it was going to be done, I would be OK with it. I'd have time to prepare. Not knowing made me uneasy. I didn't want to appear to be fearless because the man might think that I was being funny. I didn't want to be fearful either though. That made me feel weak. My choice wasn't to be killed but if I had to go, then I'd be at peace with it.

Justin stood still, he didn't make a move. I did the same. I didn't know Justin that well. I didn't know if he cared about my life or not. I mean he was a shooter, he sold drugs, he was probably lethal. I looked around the room and tried to look for a way out of this mess. I looked at Justin and he looked back at me. At first, I was confused, then after a while I figured out that he was trying to tell me something. He looked in the direction of the masked man toward his hip. I looked over and I got a good look at the gun in his belt. I looked back over at Justin and he nodded slightly. He shot at the man and while he was distracted I grabbed for the gun. Everything happened so fast. Now Justin and I were pointing guns at the masked man who was pointing his gun at us. He moved back and forth but you can tell that he was afraid. I didn't move. Justin moved closer to the man.

"What you gonna do now?"

The man began to yell. "I'll kill both of you mother fuckers, that's what I'm gonna do. You thought that you were gonna get away with what you did, huh? Nah, it's over G."

Justin looked at me again. I was becoming irritable. I knew coming here was a bad idea. Justin relaxed and began to move toward him.

The man yelled out again. "If you move any closer, I'll kill your shorty." He pointed the gun at me.

Justin remained quiet. When the masked man turned the gun toward him, I just began shooting. I just let them fly. I had never shot at anyone in my life, but I didn't know what was going to happen. This was self-defense. I shot until the clip was empty. I didn't realize how scared I was until that moment. I dropped the gun and fell to the floor. I was overwhelmed. I looked over at the man's lifeless body. Justin ran over to him, took his mask off, then looked around and made sure no one else was in the house. He looked out the windows and checked the basement. There was blood everywhere. There was blood on my clothes. There was blood on my face. I was empty. I couldn't cry but I wanted to so bad. I just killed a man. This could have all been prevented if I would have never come here. I pushed myself back against the wall and stared into space. Justin came over and sat next to me, holding me in his arms. He told me everything was OK. I knew everything wasn't OK. I didn't know what beef Justin had with him, but he's the reason for all of this. I blamed Justin for it all. It was messy, and I didn't like it. I just murdered a man because of him. He endangered my life. But this would have never happened if Justin didn't do whatever he did. I couldn't move. If I didn't know who I was before, then I definitely didn't know who I was now. I sort of blacked out. He was talking to me for a while now, but I heard nothing. I just sat still, evaluating what I had just done.

"I was scared," I confessed.

"I know. You weren't wrong."

I just sat straight faced. "Now we have to call the police, I'm going to be under investigation. I have a job, a life, I don't even live here." I began to worry.

"Don't worry about this Noel. I have everything under control."

I looked at him with question. "What do you mean? I just murdered someone. They don't care about if I was wrong or right. I just took someone's life."

Justin grabbed my hand. "I'm gonna get you cleaned up and we can go shopping. I'll get this house cleaned up and we can spend some time. You need to relax. I have everything under control." He was calm.

For a moment, I forgot that this is what he does for a living. I really do not want to be involved in this type of lifestyle. But it was much too late. I was upset. But I honestly was afraid to keep suggesting getting the police involved. Tisa had said that Justin was a loose cannon. I didn't want to see that side of him. He picked up his phone and sent a text. Almost immediately someone called, he excused himself as he talked to them. I overheard some of the conversation. He told someone he needed the situation to be cleaned up and he said the name Jerry. I figured that that was who I killed. He came back over to me and helped me off the floor. He walked me upstairs to the bathroom and helped me take off my clothes. He turned the shower on for me and reached in the linen closet for a towel and washcloth.

"Do you need help?"

I shrugged. I really didn't know. I was shaking. I wasn't sure if I could wash myself. I wasn't sure if I would miss a spot. I wasn't sure that I wouldn't pass out. I just wasn't certain. He took off his clothes and slid the shower door to the side. He walked in first then pulled me right behind him. He lathered the wash cloth and began to wash me off. Everything he did was gentle. He didn't try and have sex with me, although he naturally became aroused. He took his time and washed my entire body, he washed the blood off my skin, he washed my hands, my back. He even washed my hair. I felt as if I was floating. I felt like I had to throw up. I ran to the toilet, making a wet mess on the floor. Hunched over, I let out all of my breakfast. I felt so much better afterward. I asked if he had a toothbrush. He told me to look in the cabinet. I took the new toothbrush out of the packaging and added the crest toothpaste. That was the last thing I remembered before I passed out.

CHAPTER THIRTY-ONE

I woke up in bed. It was comfortable and soft. There was a canopy that wrapped around it where delicate, flowy curtains hung. I saw my surroundings as fluorescent objects popping out at me in my isolated dreamy world. I turned over in the bed. I was naked, my hair was wild and free, and my skin was like caramel dripping on the silk sheets. My body was sore, evidence of the tussle that I was in earlier today. My neck was pulsating from being choked, my knees were weary from being thrown to the ground. I was exhausted, and I could still taste the puke in my throat from throwing up. I looked around. I didn't see Justin. I was alone. It was quiet and peaceful, something that I had been searching for, for a long time. Even when I was home alone, I still couldn't find peace. This was good for me. All of my memories had temporarily faded away, and I was happy again. I smiled to myself and began touching the inside of my thighs. For that split second, I felt beautiful again. My skin was smooth and even though my hair was shorter, it was still soft and luxurious. I had a sudden feeling of temptation. I was soaking wet and I felt it drip between my legs. I opened them and touched myself. My kitty was pretty and bald. I had just got a wax last week in preparation of the party Clayton and I attended. I had been going crazy having sex. I had a threesome, I had a separate experience with Perez that I actually enjoyed, and Clayton and I had been intimate every time I blinked my eyes. I thought we should probably take a break. We fucked like rabbits. I was on the brink of no control. When I was with Dale, we didn't really have that much sex. He was in and out of everything: our home, our relationship, everything. I enjoyed it when it happened but not as much as I enjoyed it with Clayton, or Justin, or even Perez.

Our spark had died out. Even the last time that we were intimate, it didn't feel the same. Don't get me wrong, I was satisfied physically, but emotionally we lacked a connection that would have taken our sex from a five rating to a 10. It used to sadden me, but now I don't really care. Things were going back to normal. My concern for him had almost completely diminished, and I wasn't looking to rekindle anything with him. To be honest, he irritated me more than ever now. He was just a little too late and he didn't see the issue with any of his actions.

I began to touch my stomach, I took my pointer finger and lightly slid it up and down my skin. It tickled and sent pleasure through my body. I quietly moaned. I then touched my breast, taking that same pointer finger and gently circling it around my nipple. I slid the cover down and let the breeze hit my body. It felt good, it sent a rush through me that made me want more. At that moment, Justin knocked on the door then entered the room.

"Good morning sleeping beauty." He made his way towards me.

I looked out the bedroom window, it was dark. I looked around for my phone. "What time is it?"

"It's a little after 5:00. You've been sleep for a few hours. Your phone is on the dresser." He pointed to it.

I took a deep breath. I thought I was out for a whole day. I definitely had no intentions to stay longer than a night. I'm sure Clayton had been blowing my phone up. It's been hours since I talked to him and I forgot to tell him that I was here.

"You're a popular girl," he said to me while pulling back the curtains and sitting on the bed.

I looked at him in confusion. "Popular?"

He got up and took my phone off the dresser and handed it to me. Picking up my phone, the screen lit up with umpteen notifications. Five messages and three calls were from Clayton. The rest were between Perez, my mother, and Dale. I didn't even care that Justin was sitting there. I called Clayton back immediately. He didn't answer so I assumed that he was busy. I hung up and texted him disregarding his messages. I just let him know that I was in New York and apologized for not properly communicating with him. I told him I had got tied up in my business and that I was going to take a nap, so I would call him later. I didn't want to have a in depth discussion with him in front of Justin, it was none of his business.

I sat my phone on the bed and looked directly at Justin. He was looking out the window, I could tell that he didn't want to intrude or overstep his boundaries. He was quiet. I tapped him with my toe. He turned and kissed my foot, then took each toe individually and kissed them. He stopped then leaned over my naked body. We looked each other in the eyes and he kissed me. His kisses were warm and sweet. I felt my pussy pulsate and my nipples become erect. I began to lift his shirt and he took it all the way off between kisses. Once he was topless, I turned him on his back and began to take off his boxer briefs. He looked even bigger than before. He was hairless, the way I liked it, and he smelled of dove cocoa butter soap. His skin was rich and chocolate, flawless and neat. I was in love with the sight of him. I loved his aura and the way he carried himself, he was so clean and smooth. I sat on top of him, letting my pussy touch his belly, dripping my juices down on his skin. I leaned forward to kiss him and lifted my ass in the air. He pushed me on my back and scooted my ass closer to his face while he leaned up and began to eat. I was so sensitive, and it showed. He gripped tighter on my hips to contain me, I was all over the place. It felt so good. He made his way from up under my body to on top of me and slipped his bell head inside me. He teased me and didn't insert it all the way in. He just put the tip in and out until I pulled on his hips bringing him all the way inside me, begging for more. I let out a whimper, moving along with him, matching the rhythm of his stroke. He didn't last very long. Once he was finished, he pulled out and released in his hand. He quickly got up and went to the bathroom. I heard the faucet running and the toilet flush. When he came out he apologized for not lasting very long and laid in the bed with me. I excused myself and went to the restroom, then came back and cuddled with him. He played with my hair and looked me in my eyes. I was supposed to be letting him go, not drawing him closer. I was an idiot. This was not the plan. I murdered a man. Everything came back to me within that thought. I became sad again. A tear fell from my eyes, and he was there to wipe it away.

"It's OK, Noel. Everything is taken care of. You were acting in self-defense."

I sobbed. "I know, but that was someone's son." I couldn't stop crying.

He held me tight and wouldn't let go.

"You act like you've done this before," I said while looking him in his eyes. He looked away and back to me.

He became serious and cold. "Cut the bullshit Noel, I know you know what I do. You're a smart girl and I'm not hiding anything from you."

I was startled. I wasn't expecting that response. I began to cry harder. I didn't want to show that type of weakness, but it just came out. My heart began pumping vigorously. I was afraid.

"I know Tisa told you about me," he said sternly.

"She didn't say much," I whispered.

"Yeah alright, well you know now. If you're scared, I suggest you suck the shit up cause now you're involved." I heard his accent more than ever now.

"What do you mean I'm involved? I have nothing to do with that." I moved away from him.

"You just offed Jerry. He wasn't a direct threat to you. There was no foul play. If you would have called the boys, then you would have been taken out of here in handcuffs. Technically, I'm now an accessory to murder."

"You set me up?" I sat up abruptly.

He shook his head. "What do I have to gain from setting you up, yo? You just happened to be at the right place, at the wrong time, and took care of a light load for me. Now, I took care of everything so there is nothing you need to worry about other than keeping those pretty lips of yours shut."

I got up and began to look for my clothes then spotted them on the chair near the door. I walked toward them and began putting them on.

"Where the fuck do you think you're going?"

I ignored him and kept getting dressed. This nigga really just turned on me. He flipped shit upside down. I should have listened to Tisa. I did not want any parts of this mess. I wanted so badly to just cut things off and leave, but by the way he was acting, I was scared he would hurt me.

"I think it's best that I leave. Thank you for everything." I went back to the bed and grabbed my phone. I tried to walk to the door, but he pulled me back.

"I'm sorry, I didn't mean to flip on you. I'm just under a lot of pressure right now, Noel."

He was clearly crazy, but I played along. I saw the Lifetime movies, I knew what I had to do. I wasn't going to end up being the next dead body laid across the floor.

Justin didn't know me that well, he didn't really care about my life. I was just a good piece of ass. I let him hold me. As much as I wanted to leave, I'm sure he'd talk me into staying. I'd let him because I wanted him to think that he was in control. I know I mentioned how I needed to stop the whole control game, but in this specific situation, this is what needed to happen. I was disposable. I knew it and he knew it. Whoever cleaned up the mess from earlier could easily do the same for my body and no one would ever know. I couldn't tell him to his face that we were done, so I'd enjoy my last visit tonight and never talk to him again come tomorrow.

"Let me take you get some ice cream and shop like I promised."

I agreed, but honestly, the fact that I wanted nothing to do with him was written all over my face. If something was bothering me, it was hard to hide it. He saw it, but he ignored it. He took me to the shops at Columbus Circle and bought me a few outfits: a long dress, a track fit, some makeup, and some fragrances. He offered to buy me a bag, but I wasn't the bag type of girl. He did get me two pairs of heels and a pair of sneakers. That's what I appreciated the most, I loved shoes. While shopping, our conversation was short, I couldn't hide the fact that I was uneasy. But I made it work. He bought me some lingerie too, a white push up bra with some cheeky lace panties, a garter belt, and some knee-high stockings. Something I would wear for him tonight then burn tomorrow. I was so over him it made no sense.

We had dinner at The Sea Fire Grill, his favorite restaurant. The food was OK, but I would have rather gone to a hole in the wall. They have the best food. The rest of the night was a blur. I don't recall anything, I just remember waking up in the morning to catch a flight back to Ohio.

CHAPTER THIRTY-TWO

The flight home was cold. Something wasn't right at all. I had no prior memory of last night. The last thing I remembered was drinking at the restaurant. When I woke up, all of my bags were packed, including the new clothes I got from the shopping trip, and my purse was filled with a wad of money. I didn't even want to count it until I got home. What did he do to me? I was really afraid. I had to tell Tisa. I had to tell my mother. I had to tell somebody.

—

The first thing I did when I touched down to Cincinnati was return all my texts and calls. The first on my list was Clayton. I did not want to get him involved in this. He wasn't a street nigga and there was no way I wanted anything to happen to him because of my infidelities. I blocked Justin's number immediately and deleted everything that had anything to do with him out of my phone. I said a prayer and dialed Clayton's number. He didn't answer. I'm sure he was pissed at me for ignoring him. He wasn't stupid. I called my mom and asked her if I could stop by later tonight, we needed to talk. She said that was fine. I felt like something bad was about to happen.

I was off today but I needed to go talk to Tisa. I knew she'd be at the office, so I went home to change before heading there. I wanted to get rid of the Justin's scent.

I arrived at my house and was met by Clayton. He was sitting on the stoop waiting for me. I grabbed the bags out of my car and struggled to the door. Clearly, he was pissed. Clayton was a gentleman, there was no way he'd just let me struggle to the door with all the bags in my hand. I reached the door with both my hands full and looked at him.

"So, you were just going to go missing for a day and think everything was OK?"

I dropped my bags and just began to cry. I couldn't talk, these tears were real. I didn't know how to feel about yesterday.

He just looked at me, straight faced. "Are you going to start talking or are you going to leave me guessing? I don't want to feel like this, Noel. I'm your boyfriend. I want to be here for you. I don't want to think that you're stepping out on me. I want answers. I want to be included. I don't want us to be like this already."

I could tell that he was serious. I knew that he didn't want to see me down, and I also know that I owed him the truth. He had been nothing but good to me. I just didn't want him to react.

"Let's go inside," I said, picking my bags up off the ground.

He just sat still. "Nah, tell me now. I'm not going nowhere."

I looked him in his brown eyes and dropped my bags again. The sun was shining, and the clouds were spread sporadically throughout the sky.

"Promise me you won't react."

"I'm listening." He leaned back on the porch, spreading his legs apart, relaxing his body.

I took a deep breath. "I went to New York yesterday to break it off with a man I was dealing with. I previously went with Paisley. She wanted me to trick for some money, but I dipped on her at the party. I met this guy named Justin that night and he paid for my hotel and kept me company. We kept in touch. So yesterday he flew me out and I was supposed to break it off with him, but when I got there to one of his properties and waited on him, someone broke in. One thing led to the next, he burst in the door, and we all were holding guns to each other. I started shooting and I couldn't stop. The guy that broke in, I killed him. Justin cleaned me up because I was a nervous wreck and then I passed out. When I woke up he flipped on me and basically told me that I would go down for everything if I told because I was the one who killed the guy and when I tried to leave, he wouldn't let me. He bought me all these clothes and gave me money. He's crazy. I couldn't break it off with him, I thought he would kill me. So, I let him take me out. And the crazy thing is, I don't even know what happened last night. I think he drugged me. The last thing I remember was dinner. I should have listened to Tisa, she told me to leave him alone." I began to weep again.

"Tisa knows about this?!" He raised his voice.

I nodded. "Apparently, she was married to his uncle. She told me about him and I didn't listen. This was before you and I were together."

"So, you slept with him?"

I nodded.

"And you murdered someone?"

I nodded my head again.

"Noel how do you know this nigga won't use this shit against you? You don't even know him. What the fuck?" He shook his head and palmed his face.

"I blocked him as soon as I got here." I cried.

He grabbed my bags and helped me put them in the house. I sat on the couch thinking he'd join me. He just stood in awe.

"I don't even think I can trust you. I mean, how do I know you're not lying and playing me, huh? How do I know that you ain't trick for this shit?"

He had a valid point. I could be playing him. But I wasn't.

"I'm not playing you, but I understand if you feel like I am. I had a hard day. I don't have the energy to fight. I know I was wrong for keeping this from you and going there in the first place, and for that I apologize. But I can't take this right now." I wiped the tears from my eyes. At this point my face was puffy and sore.

"I need a few days, Noel." He kissed my forehead.

I nodded. I understood. It was selfish of me to want him to wrap his arms around me and tell me everything would be OK and that he wouldn't leave me, but that's what I wanted. I watched him walk out the door and close it behind him. I just sat in sorrow, overwhelmed in sadness and pity for myself. I looked inside my purse and counted the wad of money. I counted $5,000, all hundreds. I needed it bad. But I didn't feel comfortable taking it. I changed my clothes and headed to my mom's house with the money in my purse.

Growing up, I thought my mother hated me. The "bitches" and "hoes" she'd call me when she was drunk and mad killed me inside, even though I knew she was only mad at herself. I would never tell her that, but it did. And she would always put her husband over me. Everything he said about me, she would chime in and agree with him. I was offended. No matter how much I didn't fuck with my mama, I would never let anyone else talk shit about her. But that rule of thumb didn't apply to me. I hated her husband. I only tolerated him for her and most of the time I didn't like her either. He always had some shit to say and she'd follow him around no matter what, looking as dumb as he did. The art of submission, a substantial marriage, and a mentally ill wife.

—

Initially, I wanted to tell her what was going on, but after the talk I had with Clayton, I didn't want to repeat myself. And after more thought, I didn't want her telling my business to her husband or anyone else. She had loose lips and sometimes I don't even think she did it intentionally. Sometimes you must accept that some people will never change and that there is no reason to try to make them. I decided to keep this to myself. But I was going to drop this money to her.

She opened the door. She was lighter skinned, had long silky soft straight hair, and was slim thick like me. I'm assuming she forgot that I was coming. She was dressed in a brown midi off the shoulder dress and some gold heels. She looked so happy.

"Oh, I forgot you were coming. Me and Courtney are about to go out."

She was always so happy to go out with him because all he did was do her dirty. Him taking her out was her way of showing his side bitches that she was still around. It was proof to herself that he still loved her. And he probably did, but sometimes people love you with thoughts or words but not actions. She was such a goofy, it made me sick.

"I don't want to hold you, I just wanted to bring you something." I took out the money and placed it in her hand. She looked down at it and her mouth dropped.

"What's this Noel?" She was in shock, trying to whisper. Although she was the "perfect wife," when my mother came across money, she kept her mouth closed.

I patted her hand and closed it. "You deserve it."

Her face was red, and her eyes teared up. This was the first time that I have ever genuinely seen my mom happy in years. Not the temporary happy that would wear off by the end of the night, the happy that held weight and longevity. I wanted her to take it and put together a fund to leave Courtney's ass, but I knew that wasn't going to happen. What she did with the money was none of my business. This was just my way of forgiving the unsaid and moving on. She was my mother at the end of the day, and she made a lot of sacrifices for me that I'm sure I knew nothing about. Everyone makes mistakes. There isn't a rulebook to parenting, I'm sure she did the best that she could. At this moment, all I wanted her to do was be happy.

"Take yourself shopping, or to the spa, get your hair and nails done. Do something for yourself for once. OK, Stephanie?"

She nodded and put the money in her satchel. She mouthed "thank you." I smiled and walked back to my car. Something about that felt right. Any other time I would have used all the harbored feelings toward her as an excuse to keep the money all for myself. But something told me that she needed it more than I did. This was the end of my ill feelings for her, this was the end of the tension, and this was a new beginning for both of us.

These last few days made me realize what was important to me in my life, and she was definitely one of those things. Through the good and bad, she was always there for me. Even when I felt alone, even when I didn't want to talk to her, even when she was going through her own issues, she was always there and for that I was thankful. I wanted to show her that she was loved despite the cold shoulder I gave her at times. I was healing too. We had to heal together and stick by each other's side. I honestly felt as though my mother was the only person I had right now. I hurt myself holding grudges towards her and I wasn't benefiting from it in any way. So, I let that hurt go. Life is short. I don't want to remember my mom in any bad way and the same goes for her. If one of us was to leave this earth tomorrow, I didn't want our thoughts of each other to be tainted.

I walked lighter when I left there. The hurt was gone, and the pain was at ease. Now I had a lot more to do.

CHAPTER THIRTY-THREE

I sat in the car in front of the office building. I saw Tisa's car, so I knew that she was there. For some reason, I didn't feel like going to talk to her anymore. I had already drove all the way here, so I was going to go in even if I had to make myself. I just needed time to breathe.

The rain slowly dropped on my windshield. The skies grew darker and I grew weary at the thought of getting out of the car. I wanted to go home. I didn't feel safe. I was paranoid and honestly, I had this crazy thought that Justin was going to try and kill me. My phone began to ring, it was Dale. I let it ring. I definitely didn't want to talk to him. I hated the thought of him. I couldn't seem to come to peace with him or why he treated me the way he did. When it came to him, all I did was wonder why. He was a manipulator so just asking him wouldn't suffice. He texted me right after his call went to voicemail. The message stated that this was his last time reaching out and that his current girlfriend, his child's mother, did in fact want to meet me. She wanted me to come to dinner tonight. Apparently, she had some things she wanted to get off her chest as well and she also wanted some closure. I texted him back, I gave in. I was going to go. Maybe it would be good for me. Then right after I would wash my hands clean of the situation. Usually messy situations like these gave me bad vibes. Something about this made me feel like it would ease my mind. Hopefully so, because this was one of the things that bothered me the most. I couldn't help but feel like I wasn't good enough, no matter how these niggas made me feel. I wasn't confident and even though I hid it very well, it equally bothered the fuck out of me. I cut my hair and had to cope with not being myself or what I was used to. Change was good, but this made me reconstruct from ground up and have to rebuild my self-esteem. I had no moral support. I didn't have any friends. Paisley was the only one and you see how that's currently going. I didn't trust anyone, and most of all, I no longer trusted myself.

I got out of the car with the same floating feeling that I had all day. I felt like I was coming down from a high. I felt trippy as fuck and I know I didn't smoke or take any drugs. This was something I couldn't shake. It had almost been a full day since I returned to Cincinnati, and I felt so out of it. I thought I was going crazy. I was listening to my body and something was wrong. I arrived at the door of the office and opened it with my key. I made it known that I was there and walked into Tisa's office. She was actively editing a script. She was quiet, but she welcomed me in.

"What's up, Noel? I feel like I haven't seen you in forever."

She was right, it had been a while since I had seen her but that's only because I came in when she was off or out of the office.

"I need to talk to you," I said with all seriousness in my face as I shut the door and sat down. We were the only two there, but I still wanted to be safe. She looked up from her work and tipped her glasses low. She was silent, waiting for me to speak.

"I know you told me not to continue with Justin, so I went to break it off with him…"

She just continued to look at me. "And?"

"Well, he flew me out to New York and it didn't go so well." I played with my fingernails while I talked, trying not to pick the scabs on my arms, a horrible habit that I picked up recently. She was attentive, but still quiet so I proceeded.

"I think he did something to me. I feel weird. I feel like he drugged me or something. I don't know, I've never been drugged but I feel high and I can't come down. I haven't drunk or taken anything at all. I'm so confused."

She palmed her face with her hand, took a deep breath then looked me in the eyes trying to hold back tears. "Noel, tell me what happened please. Everything. It's OK, I won't judge you, I want to help." She maneuvered her rolling chair around her desk and sat closer to me, grabbing my hand.

I let out a sigh and then continued. "Well, I'm not sure if you know, but me and Clayton are a thing now. I went to tell Justin that I could no longer deal with him, you know because I have a boyfriend. He had me go to one of his properties and wait on him while he finished up with a client. I waited and ended up falling asleep. Then out of nowhere, I heard a loud noise. Everything happened so fast. I went to the kitchen and there was a masked man that grabbed me and choked me up. Justin finally burst through the doors."

Tisa interrupted. "Was the house brick? What color was it?"

"Ummm…the house was brick, and it had a black door. I remember now. It had some nice interior décor."

"What happened after he burst through the door?"

"So, the man threw me on the ground and they had guns pointed at each other and me. I ended up grabbing the other gun from the man's waist and we were all pointing them at each other. I was scared, I didn't know what to do. I just started shooting. I killed the man, Tisa." I began crying again. I was so upset. I had so many emotions tied to this fuck up. I never in my life hurt anyone, so murdering someone really had me open and vulnerable. I was really losing it. At first, I thought I would be OK, but now I was beginning to second guess myself.

She hugged me tight like a mother would hug her child when she didn't know what to say.

"I told Clayton because he thought that I was blowing him off for a whole day, and now I think he's going to break up with me. It's too much. I can't deal with this. I shouldn't have gone there. I should have just blocked him and kept it moving. I didn't think this would happen. Then he took me shopping and gave me money," I said, still weeping.

Tisa didn't look surprised. "You did right. I wouldn't have objected to anything he offered, he is seriously dangerous. I know you're scared. I'm here. I've been through all of this before. It pains me to see him following in his uncle's footsteps. Get rid of that money, Noel."

"I gave it to my mother."

"Good, now burn those clothes and check your bags and shoes, your phone too. Make sure there is no tracker on you or microphone. I'll go with you." She quickly grabbed her paperwork and put it in her bag. "I'll follow you to your house so we can look together and if you want, you can stay with me for a few days." She was acting like he was going to come looking for me. This scared me even more.

"I want to stay with Clayton. I appreciate your offer, I do, but I need to make things right with him." He was upset, he needed his space, but I also didn't want to give him too much space. I missed him and being around him is all I wanted to do right now.

"No!" She almost screamed. "OK, let me help you understand who you're dealing with, babe. He's ruthless. He will hurt anyone in his way. I'm sure you don't want Clayton involved. I don't want Clayton involved. Shit, I don't want you involved." She was starting to shake, dropping her car keys on the ground. She took a deep breath. "Have you returned any calls or anything from him?"

"No, I blocked him this morning. But, tonight if I stay with you, I have to go make a stop first. It shouldn't take long."

"You really should try and reschedule until this gets handled. But go ahead."

"Gets handled? What are you going to do, Tisa?" I was seriously intrigued. I've known this woman for years, she didn't strike me as the type to take that type of action.

"Just know I'm going to handle it," she said, opening her office door and leading me out. I said nothing else. I was too overwhelmed. We walked out to my car and before I got back inside, she did a thorough inspection, just to make sure the car wasn't wired. I hopped inside, and she followed me to the condo. We searched the entire house and found nothing. She took the clothes with her in her car and said we could burn them at her house in her fireplace. I checked my messages and Dale sent me the address to his new home. I responded and let him know that I would be on my way soon. Before leaving, Tisa gave me a spare key to her place and sent me her address.

Clayton was on my mind heavy. I called him, no answer. I usually don't, but I left him a message. I wanted him to know that I cared about him and I didn't want to be shut out like this. I followed up with a text message asking him to call me back. I hope he would. I hope that this wasn't the end of us. Honestly, this was just bad timing. I got caught up in so much nonsense and I'm starting to think I should have just stayed to myself. I was in search of love and attention, I found them both in the wrong places. To analyze the situation, this is probably my karma. I cheated on my boyfriend. No matter what he did to me, that wasn't right. I had to live with what I did. And I feel like I'm paying for it now.

I sat in the car for a few minutes before pulling off and thought to myself how differently things would have turned out if I had never cheated or went out with Clayton. How different things would be if I never would have gone to the Marriot or even found out that Dale had a baby on me. Would I still be going to bed and waking up alone? Would I still feel empty inside? What would my relationship with Clayton be? Would I have ever met Justin or went out with Paisley? Would we still be friends? Would I have ever met Perez and became intimate with her? It's crazy how one thing can set off a chain of events. I rolled up my window and lit a joint that I had sitting in the ashtray. I had to get high before going over there, or I was going to be stressed out by the time I left. I needed to mellow out, even though I still sort of felt high from before. I needed something to relax my mind. I was on constant go since I got back in the city, and I felt like I just needed rest. My eyes hurt, I had a forehead headache, and I was just over today. Hopefully the weed would help. I was a casual smoker but the more shit I went through, the more I did it.

As I inhaled the smoke, I thought about what could have possibly happened when I blacked out. I tried to remember but I couldn't visualize anything. The possibilities of what could have happened to me the night before I left New York clouded my mind. All I could see was me shooting the masked man to death and Justin having his way with me. Or worse, letting his friends have their way with me. I saw stories like that all the time on Lifetime and the news. I didn't want to be that girl. I really didn't. But who knows what went down, and I honestly didn't want to find out. I would be shattered if I was taken advantage of like that. So, I had to come to peace with it and move forward.

—

This was going to be interesting. I had no idea what to expect from this visit with Dale and his child's mother. I looked to see what part of town I was headed to on the GPS. They lived in West Chester, which was interesting. I wonder who's house it was. Did he pay the bills? Or did she already stay there? My mind took a turn. What if he was setting me up? I texted him and asked if this was a set up and he called me almost instantly. I answered, not happy to speak to him.

"Yes?"

"Set up?! Are you going crazy? Noel, if you don't want to come then don't. I just want to clear some things up and she does too. What the hell are you on right now? I would never try to 'set you up.' The fuck?"

He was offended, but I didn't care. With all the shit that had been going on, I just wanted to make sure that I was safe. I wanted to say that I knew he wouldn't do anything like that, but recent activities had me second guessing everything. I just said OK, then he hung up. At this point I was high. I had it in my mind that I was going over there and then going to Tisa's to crash. I had a few things to do in the office tomorrow and I knew I'd be exhausted.

I pulled up to a newly built home, Dale's suburban was sitting outside, and a Benz was parked right next to it. He was either spending some bread on her, or she had her own. I can't lie, I was a little jealous. Maybe that's why he gave her a baby. She could handle things on her own. I know Dale made money, but not this much. He couldn't support me and her with what he made and still have extra and support a child. I sent him a text before spraying myself with some cheap perfume that I kept in the car, so I wouldn't smell too loud. I got out the car and fixed my clothes. I had on a pink sweat suit that I got from H&M, some pink Huaraches and a pink head wrap. I didn't bother putting on makeup, I just wasn't up to it today.

She opened the door with the baby in her arms. "Hey love, nice to finally meet you! You can take a seat at the table in the dining room to your left. We'll be right in."

I couldn't believe that I was sitting in the house of my ex boyfriend's mistress. She was cute, short with long natural hair. She was thick, and I mean really thick. It looked like she had a solid D cup and she had a really nice natural ass. Of course, there was a little belly fat, she just had a baby, but overall, she looked really good. She had a really sweet slightly high-pitched voice. I can see why he liked her. Hell, I liked her. I definitely saw a pattern in Dale's preference. He had a type for sure. The natural everything type of chick. The professional, bourgeois type. Shit, he had dough, why court a bitch that had nothing to offer? He made his money and handled his business. I liked that about him, but he was still a man, and unfortunately, I had it set in my mind that all men cheat. Whether or not that was true, I don't know, but that's the way I see it. They all cheat at least once. Hopefully after this sitting we can conclude this situation and get some closure. All of us, including him.

I sat at the table and waited. I could smell food being prepared, it smelled like steak and potatoes. I loved a good medium well steak, but I didn't eat it that often. I wasn't a heavy meat eater. Dale came into the room and interrupted my thoughts.

"What's up, Noel?" He sat down across from me.

"What's up? I love this house. She's pretty. I see why you like her." I wasn't being bitter, I was being honest. I'm sure he didn't take it that way though.

"So are you…" he began awkwardly. "She made steak, potatoes, and some asparagus, your favorite," he said looking down at his hands.

"Why am I here?" I was upfront. I wasn't really in the mood to play games. I just wanted to get to the point and leave.

"I wanted to talk to you, face to face, about everything that happened. And make you an offering."

His mistress walked around the corner of the kitchen with two plates in her hand. She sat one in front of me and the other in front of him. I began to thank her and then thought about the fact that he said he wanted to make me an offer.

"An offer?"

His mistress nodded her head yes and told me to hold on a second. She went into the kitchen and grabbed another plate for herself. She sat down next to Dale and said her prayers to herself and began. She was definitely a wife. I didn't do half the things she did in one sitting. I was busy with school and work. Everything made sense now.

"I didn't introduce myself before, my name is Milani. I'm a special agent for the CSI."

I just looked at her in disbelief. She didn't give me that impression. I thought she was a housewife to be honest.

She continued. "First and foremost, I apologize for intruding your home and having dealings with Dale. He told me that he had someone and at the time, I didn't care. I can go on and on about what I was going through but when it comes down to it, I was wrong, and I apologize," she said to me then looked at Dale.

Dale chimed in. "I also was wrong, and I apologize. I know how what I did affected you emotionally and I can't take it back, but I am terribly sorry."

I had no words. I mean, I honestly didn't know what to say. I was a little bothered because now I knew that she knew all about me, even though it wasn't her responsibility to respect my relationship. I just didn't get why they invited me here and what offer she was trying to make. I just nodded my head. At this point, I was trying my best not to be rude and nasty because I wanted to let both of them have it.

"OK, I'm past that. So, what are you offering?" I lost my appetite and was extremely annoyed. I sipped my water and waited for the offer.

"We want you to be a part of our family."

I instantly spit out my water and began to laugh. They both sat with serious faces.

"Oh, you were serious. Um, yeah, no. Actually, I think it's best that I go. I understand and appreciate both of your apologies and I accept them, but I'm not with the whole joining families thing. Just not my style. Dale, you should know that. Thank you so much for the meal but unfortunately, I've lost my appetite. Thank you so much. I have to go."

I grabbed my purse and got up from the chair, pushing it in politely. Dale and Milani were both asking me to stay, but I just couldn't do it. I was so insulted that I was on the verge of tears. I couldn't sit there for much longer. It was too much. I ran out of the house and got inside the car, pulling off immediately. I thought to go back home and grab a few things.

If I was going to be staying at Tisa's, I needed more clothes.

Who knows how long I'd be at her house.

CHAPTER THIRTY-FOUR

I drove thirty minutes back to my house and sat in the driveway. I finally stopped and took a deep breath. I thought I would be OK, but the tears just came pouring down. My phone was ringing off the hook and I just wanted peace and quiet, just for five minutes, maybe 10.

My street was always dark and the light I had by the door was out. I needed to breathe again before going inside. I needed to regroup and namaste. My moods were all over the place; one minute I was happy, the next I was upset, one minute I was ready to risk it all, the next minute I wanted to crawl back in a hole and prosper. I couldn't deal with myself. I honestly thought I was losing my mind. My emotions ate at me all day long and when they didn't, I was numb. I thought about going to talk to someone but quickly decided against it. I didn't like people in my personal life, especially ones who didn't understand. I feel like therapists capitalize off our money and don't really know how to fix anything or properly listen. The suggestions that I've heard from therapists were either super extreme or too passive, so collectively, I think going to one is just a bad idea. Honestly, I rather die with my secrets than tell someone else that I was struggling. The battle of the mind was serious, but I know I can overcome it one day at a time. Or at least that's what I wanted to believe.

I got out the car, leaving my purse and belongings behind, and walked to the door. I was high as shit and walked off balance, almost dropping my keys and my phone. This was starting to be a problem. When I was feeling down and out or stressed, I turned to alcohol and marijuana. I kept telling myself to slow down but I couldn't. I got lost in substances I thought would neutralize my mood when in reality, it threw me into deeper depression. The shit was getting old. I told myself I'd stop tomorrow. I don't need anything to make me feel better, I needed to be sober, and be able to think clearly. Maybe my decisions wouldn't be so impulsive and fucked up.

As I reached the door, I heard someone beside me in the bushes. I looked to my right and there was a tall slim dark man. He looked familiar. It was Justin. Immediately, I reached for my phone to call 911, Tisa, Clayton, anybody, because I knew something about this wasn't right. But I was so afraid that I dropped my phone on the ground in the process.

"You might wanna tighten up," he said with a smirk across his face.

I wasn't amused. "What do you want? Don't you think showing up here like this is a little creepy?"

He was wild. I blocked his number and the same night he shows up at my house unannounced. And what makes it even worse is he's never even been here before. So now I was wondering if he really did have a tracker or a camera on me. Or worse, had someone watching.

"I just want to talk. I called you, but someone has me blocked." I moved closer to the door. "So, you show up at my house unannounced? How did you even know where I lived?" I was reaching for my phone.

He cocked his gun back and began to pull the trigger. I looked up at him in awe.

"Really?"

He nodded and walked toward me with the gun to my head. "You're going to come with me, and we are going to handle some business. Perez works for me by the way. So next time you feel so free to include her in your extra-curricular activities, you should run it by me." He pushed me toward the end of the driveway, knocking my phone out of my hand to the concrete. I tried to pick it up, but he wasn't going for that.

I walked with him to the all-black Hummer that he had his driver pick me up in, and waited for him to open the door. This is why people say not to be so trustworthy of men you don't know. From my first encounter with Justin, I would have never guessed that he was this way. I would have never thought that Perez was a spy. I instantly regretted inviting her over my house and introducing her to my boyfriend. I don't know what they had planned for Clayton, but I grew weary thinking about it. I wanted to contact Tisa and give her a heads up, but I couldn't. Justin opened the car door and just as I was about to climb in; boom, there was black.

—

I woke up naked, chained to a bed. The bed was old and smelled of sex. I looked around the room and saw no windows, one door, white walls, and a small table with food. What the fuck was going on? At this point, all I could think about was dying. I had horrific thoughts of him killing me and no one knowing. I hope Tisa found my phone and realized that I was abducted and came to my rescue. I didn't know what time or day it was. All I knew was my head was aching and I couldn't remember why. The room was empty and silent. I couldn't help but think I was having a horrible nightmare that I couldn't wake up from. What could I have done to deserve any of this. I lived my life in fear of bad karma, and here I was in a horrible situation with no means to understand why. All I kept thinking about was why. Why me? I wasn't a grimy person. I wasn't scandalous. I wasn't *that* person. I wonder who I was and what

I did in my past life. Maybe that's why I was here. Either way, I didn't want to die like this. Tears formed and began to fall down my face, then the door opened, and Justin walked in. He had on a grey sweat suit and had a syringe in his hand filled with a light brown fluid. I began to move around abruptly. I screamed but no one came to save me. The room was quiet and still. I had no idea what he was doing so when he grabbed my hand, I squirmed around trying to break free.

"I'll do anything you want just let me go!" I pleaded.

He was silent as he waited for me to calm down and felt for a vein. "You're going to do what I want anyway," he said as he injected the fluid in my vein, then let me go. He walked toward the door, looked back at me, then closed it.

A few minutes passed, and I began to feel a sudden rush of pleasure. My toes began to curl, and my vagina was dripping wet. The breeze in the room made me excited and I began to think of the sexual experiences I had in the last six months. Then the door opened again, and a tall dark man entered. He was slim and built, he had a baby face, and looked a little familiar. He closed the door and made his way in the room, turning the light off. I wanted to be scared but I was so excited,

I laid there in a trance. I couldn't see anything but a silhouette. He moved closer and closer to me, then began to kiss and suck on my toes. I couldn't control myself. My body moved in all types of directions. He then made his way up to my pussy. He leaned in and licked my clit three times and stuck his penis in. Everything happened so fast. I knew this wasn't right, but I enjoyed every bit of it. I became so wet and let out so many moans. He was so big and fat, he felt so good as he filled me up. He unchained me and turned me over to have his way with me. Something was wrong. I didn't know who this man was, and I didn't want to be intimate with him, but my body said otherwise. He thrusted faster and harder into me and finally I felt a warm substance enter my walls. Then he left me there in the dark alone. My high began to come down and I was drowsy. I wanted to go to sleep, but I couldn't move. One by one, different men came into that little room and had their way with me. I was all fucked out. I wanted a nap and a warm shower. My body was sore as fuck, and I didn't have the strength to get up or do anything. I was a puppet. I wanted to escape but physically, I couldn't. Justin let whoever do what they wanted to me, and I couldn't do anything about it. I began to cry until I fell asleep, wondering what tomorrow would bring.

CHAPTER THIRTY-FIVE

In my head, there were whispers of Justin giving me an ultimatum and whispers of Paisley apologizing to me, but I couldn't make out for what exactly. My head still ached. In the back of my mind, I made out street sounds and birds chirping. I opened my eyes and I realized that I was outside of my house laying on the stoop. My phone was sitting next to me and my keys were in my hand. What the fuck. Shit was trippy lately and I can't decipher my dreams from reality. I had the same feeling I had when coming home from New York when I killed that poor man. My feet were light, and I felt high. I tried to stand up and quickly came tumbling back down. OK, let me regroup and try again. My vagina ached like it had been active all night long. My stomach was filled with sharp pains and my entire body was sore. I picked up my phone and saw that Tisa had called me 10 times. No calls, from Clayton. And there was one call from Dale. I got up, successfully this time, and caught my balance. My car was parked in the same place it was before. I went to unlock my door and it was already open. My house was trashed. There was shit thrown everywhere, the kitchen table was knocked over, and there was something black all over my walls. I stepped back and closed the door, then slid back down to the ground and began to cry. I didn't know what to do. I didn't care to find out who did that to my condo and at this point I was over life in general. I picked up my phone and dialed Tisa's number and waited for it to ring. A white Tesla pulled in the driveway, it was Tisa. Hanging up the phone I got up and walked toward the car. She hopped out and ran to me making sure I was OK.

"I told you not to come back here! Are you alright?" She sounded like a worried parent.

"Yeah I'm good. I need to lay down. The house is trashed. I don't know who did it or how, but it's trashed. Oh, I need to grab my purse out my car." I quickly walked toward my truck, opened the door, and grabbed my bag. I checked it to make sure no one put anything in it or took anything from it. Everything was still in place. I looked up and Tisa was walking into my condo looking around. I really didn't want to go in there, the sight made me want to throw up. I felt so sick to my stomach. I opened her door and sat my stuff inside then made my way to my front door. I couldn't just let her go in there alone.

"Tisa?" I called her name walking up the steps.

I walked into my room and there was glass everywhere.

"Noel, we have to go." She grabbed my hand, and ran down the steps, dragging me with her.

"What's going on? Why do we have to leave?"

She ignored me and continued on the path to her car with my hand in hers. We got to her car and we both got in.

"I can't tell if the things happening are real or fake. I don't know if I'm dreaming when these horrible things go on or if they're reality. My head hurts so bad and my body aches. I feel like I'm coming off a high. My vagina is sore, and when I close my eyes I remember Justin shooting something in my veins, and me just going wild. So many men had their way with me. I keep hoping it isn't true, but the way I feel, just makes me believe these things happened. I just woke up in front of my house. I know I saw him last night, I know I did. He pushed me I dropped my phone. I just don't understand. Why didn't you tell me Tisa?" I cried to her hysterically. I looked over and she kept her eyes on the road. There were tears in her eyes as she spoke.

"When I hired you, I saw you as a younger me. Except, when I was your age, I was boy crazy. I ended up meeting Robert and at first, he was everything. He made me feel like I had been missing out. He bought me what I wanted and took me wherever. He gave me the finest things." She smiled to herself. "He married me and moved me in, I stayed in New York for a few months. After a while, he came home later and later, and things changed but I couldn't figure out why. He was in the streets heavy, that's how he put food on our table. So, I asked him to invest in me. I knew my days with him would be coming to an end soon. Don't ask how I knew, I just had a feeling. He gave me $20,000 and I paid up my rent for my house here for a year, then created some of my own short films and submitted them to a few companies. An investment company reached out to me; they wanted me to direct and do some sets for some feature films. I set up my own home here and Robert didn't know anything about it. Well, until a friend of mine ran back and told him."

"Why would she do that?" I interrupted.

"Because she was pregnant with his baby." She continued driving.

"Wow. That's scandalous as fuck," I said, trying to figure out where she was going with this story.

"They had been sleeping together since before I met him, and she never told me. When I found out, he acted like he didn't even know her, just to keep me around. Of course, I didn't agree with him shunning his baby, but he wanted nothing to do with her or the child. I didn't want anything to do with any of them. But Robert was and is still a very dangerous man. So, I slowly prepared to move back to Ohio permanently.

I cut her off and things with him and I went back to normal in his eyes. Then one day, he found out about my home in Cincinnati. I came home thinking I was going to be away from him and he was sitting in my living room with Justin who was just a toddler at that time. I was terrified. I felt like I'd always fail when it came to running away from him. He said he loved me and he didn't ever want me to leave. He'd do whatever it took to get me back. I felt trapped and alone. My only friend was the one he impregnated. Then I started to feel bad because I wouldn't even look at her, but I'd still deal with him regularly.

"So, I reached out and we made amends. She didn't have any family or anyone else that was alive that could help her if she needed it. So, when she was stressed out, she came to stay with me. After all, I forgave her and was truly at peace with the situation. Robert and Justin went back and forth between here and New York until my friend's baby was born. Then he swore he'd keep Justin away from him. It was a boy. He looked just like him. I was there with her when she gave birth. I was there when she needed someone to support her. I was his daddy. And then one day, she didn't come home. Her car was gone but her belongings were still there. I called and called and called her, but her phone was dead. I left messages, no response. So, I took care of her child, her beautiful baby boy. I asked Robert to help me look for her and he told me no. He had seen the baby, but refused to interact with him. He didn't sign the birth certificate either. I thought he was so stupid. I was fed up and wanted out. So, I asked my mother to watch the baby and flew out to New York. Since she had the baby, he didn't really visit. He stayed in New York. I rarely saw him unless we went out here, but he didn't come to the house because she was there with *his* child."

"So, wait, you didn't think they were still messing around?"

"Honey, I didn't care. I stayed married to him because I was afraid, not because I still loved him."

"Did you ever find your friend."

She nodded. "When I got to New York, I went to visit my sister. We weren't close, but I had to tell someone because I truly thought he was going to end up killing me. Her boyfriend at the time was Robert's rival. She planned to tell him and take care of everything. I'd been around him long enough to know that that wasn't going to be as easy as it seemed. I knew the street life. My father was killed in the streets. I stopped her and asked her to tell no one unless I asked.

"I pulled up to one of his properties and he wasn't there, but Justin was with one of his homeboys who was watching him. I heard someone crying and whimpering from the basement. I went in the direction and it got louder and louder. There were four rooms filled with strung out women, being forced to give up their bodies. One of them was my friend, the mother of his child. I tried to save her." Tisa began crying hysterically. "She wouldn't leave with me. I tried to save her. She just kept saying, 'take care of my baby, take care of my baby.' Then she took her last breath. She overdosed right there in front of me. I took a video of what I saw just in case I needed it later. I tiptoed up the steps and snuck out of the house without anyone noticing and went back to my sisters with the video I took. Then I left and went back to Ohio."

I began to cry. Now it all made sense.

"I went home and served him divorce papers. He never came back to Ohio, but he sends me flowers and refuses to sign. I raised her son and when I finally told him about everything, he was eighteen. He moved away out of resentment, and I don't blame him." She said.

"I'm worried about Clayton, what if they find him," I said interrupting her.

"He won't bother Clayton."

"How do you know?! We have to go warn him. I got him into this mess," I screamed.

"Noel, Clayton is his son!"

I sat in silence. Everything made so much sense now. Why she wanted me to hook up with him, why Clayton reacted the way he did when he found out what I was doing in New York. I felt so played.

"Another thing, I been doing some research, Paisley set you up. Tommy works under Justin and having you at that party was all in his plan. Perez also works for Justin. That's how he knew where to find you. Tommy is Paisley's boyfriend," she said pulling up to Enterprise Rent-A-Car.

I've been getting played by everyone this entire time. Justin told me about Perez but the rest of this was all brand new to me. There were so many secrets, it made my head hurt. I would have rather stayed with Dale and been a part of his family than deal with any of this. My perfect life had been flipped upside down.

She got out of the car and told me she would be back. I just sat still and waited. I had no idea what I'd do next. It seemed like I was stuck. I didn't know who trashed my house, I didn't know where Clayton was, and I didn't know if Justin would come back for me or not. I had to think fast.

Tisa came back to the car and handed me a key. "Drive this from now on. I need you to go stay with Dale while I take care of Justin."

I took the keys and looked to the left, there was a small black Nissan Altima beside us. She got me a rental.

"You need to stay off the scene as much as possible. I'll talk to Clayton, he just needs some time. Here," she said, handing me a burner phone. "Use this. Put all the numbers that you need in it and give me your phone."

I entered Dale's number, her number, my mom's, and Clayton's number, then gave her my phone. She took it and got out the car and stepped on it, destroying it.

"I called Dale and let him know what was going on, he's expecting you. Justin's going to come back for you, I need you out the way until I reach Robert and can get this taken care of."

I got out the car and grabbed my bags. My head was spinning at this point. I called Dale and told him I was on my way and watched Tisa pull out of the Enterprise parking lot. I then started the car and pulled off in the direction of Dale's house and dialed my mom's number.

"Hey Noel!" She sounded so happy.

"Hey mom, what are you doing?" I was trying to hide my tears.

"I'm baking right now. What's going on?" She sounded concerned. I haven't called her mom in years.

"Nothing, just wanted to see how you've been. Have you done anything special for yourself?" I was curious.

"Yes! I went shopping and got my hair and toes done. Thank you so much baby! I really appreciate you!"

I smiled inside when she said that. My mother wasn't the type to ask questions. I didn't have to explain where I got the money.

"Oh, honey I have to go. Courtney just got home. We have to run to the store. I love you." "I love you too," I said hanging up.

I connected my phone to the Bluetooth and blasted some old school Sade. I wasn't even a fan of her, but I needed something to ease my mind and help me relax.

Let's see, in the past six months, my home was torn apart, my boyfriend had a secret family, I went wild and gave myself to multiple men, one of them is trying to kill me and put me in the sex trade, one of them is the other's cousin, my best friend set me up, and I slept with her friend who is the spy for the nigga who's trying to put me in the sex trade. Oh, and I'm on my way to my ex's house that wants me to be a part of his family. My life was all over the place. I called Clayton.

"What Noel?"

"Hello?" I was surprised he answered. "Yes, I just wanted to tell you I love you." I waited for a response.

"I love you too, but I need time. Tisa is going to figure everything out. I've talked to Dale and he gave me his word to not bother you."

"When is everyone having all these conversations without me? I'm so weirded out."

"Relax, Tisa called around last night looking for you. We all talked and figured out a plan. Dale's new girl is with the CSI, she's going to take them down. Don't even worry about that. Just get there and out of sight." He was stern.

"I love you so much," I told him again.

"I love you too," he said and hung up.

I turned my music back up. The tears came back to back. I was so overwhelmed, I couldn't stop. I didn't need them all worrying about me. I didn't need them risking their lives for me. I had to end this.

I thought of all my past experiences and remembered when I felt like I was walking on water and was so happy and filled with joy. I didn't think about the bad or worry about the things out of my control. Things were great there. I wanted to feel like that again. Warm, at home, and joyous.

I was on the highway headed north. Dale lived in West Chester, I had about twenty minutes until I reached his exit. I thought about my mom, I thought about Dale, I thought about

Journee and Milani, I thought about Clayton, and I thought about Tisa. I even thought about Justin. I wonder what cruel thing took place in his life to make him feel like he had to take advantage of women and sell their bodies. I thought about Robert, who I never met. He had to be a traumatized individual to do the same thing. I thought about Jonathan too. I wonder what he was doing. And I thought about my future. I thought about Perez. I forgave her. She was just doing her job. And Paisley, Lord knows I was hurt, but I forgive her. I forgave them all, and I hope they would forgive me.

Everything was thrown off by the thought of multiple men having their way with me. My body, I need a new one. My spirit is low, and my soul feels like it was sold to the highest bidder. I don't feel like myself anymore. I just want to feel liberated; free of worry and hurt, free of lasting impressions on people who don't care about me, and free of sorrow. I said a prayer and looked up and down the highway. There wasn't anyone coming from behind me, so I slowly hit a U turn. My adrenaline rushed as I sped up all the way to 100 miles per hour. I saw a semi-truck try to speed around me, but it was much too late. The world around me was silent, calm, and dark. I arrived.

CHAPTER THIRTY-SIX

There were trees the color of lavender and fields of magenta, orange, red, and neon blue flowers. The skies were orange and the clouds were white. I frolicked around and laid gently across the fluffy ground. There was a warm feeling from inside me, taking over my body. I could finally think clearly. I was breathing fresh air and taking my time experiencing the foreign things around me. The butterflies sang sweet songs that made me shout and rejoice. The snakes slithered away to the cabanas that sat in front of the beach where the waves crashed on the shore of pink sand. I was home. I began to sing, filling the land with life. I ran into the waves and indulged in the refreshing water. The dolphins swam around me and created a whirlpool where a mermaid came to the surface. She looked a lot like me. She didn't say a word, but I knew to follow her. I swam to the middle of the whirlpool where she grabbed my hand and hugged me. She told me that she had been waiting and she was going to take me somewhere she knew I would love. I held my breath and we sunk below the water so deep that the water evaporated. I saw an island, pretty as the ones in Bora Bora, but better. There were trees of fruit, vegetables, nuts, and animals, all waiting for me. I had long hair again and I was dressed in a long flowing dress. I know all good things come to an end, but for now, I was satisfied. I was lost in liberation. I was free.